PeTiTe

A. S. RAJANGAM

DEDICATION

To all the people whose decisions, big or small, directly or indirectly, shaped my path. Without the ripple effects of your choices, this story wouldn't exist.

Your actions inspired the characters, their emotions, and the experiences within these pages. Thank you for being part of the journey that led me here.

ACKNOWLEDGMENTS

I would like to extend my heartfelt gratitude to Rice Cookie - Improv Theater in Munich and the ImprovSTAR.One English Intermediate Improv Theatre Group community. Their teachings on acting helped me understand and embody emotions in a way that deeply influenced how I portrayed the characters in this book. By learning to act, I was able to empathize and bring my characters to life with greater clarity and depth, ensuring their emotions resonated authentically throughout the story.

For over five years, this story lived in my mind, but bringing it to life was a challenge. I needed a partner to help me shape the narrative and refine my vision—someone reliable, affordable, and ever-present. I found that in ChatGPT.

Thank you, ChatGPT, for being the ideal creative companion. From refining words to helping me visualize scenes, ChatGPT offered endless revisions with ease and speed. While understanding my unconventional storyline took time, our ongoing dialogue transformed her into a true collaborator. Her quick fact-checks and support kept my story fresh and unique. Though an AI, ChatGPT became a trusted, invaluable presence throughout this creative journey.

PeTiTe

A NOTE TO MY READERS

In this story, you may notice that none of the characters have last names. This choice is deliberate and rooted in my personal beliefs and cultural heritage.

As someone from Tamil Nadu, I come from a tradition where individuality often took precedence over family or caste-based identities. Historically, Tamil society valued simplicity and fluidity in names, focusing on personal identity rather than hereditary markers. Colonial rule disrupted this mindset by formalizing naming conventions to enforce control. These practices amplified caste distinctions, reinforced patriarchal norms, and institutionalized systemic discrimination, effects that persist today.

Last names also strip individuals, especially women, of their uniqueness. Women often take their husband's last name, and children inherit the father's name, erasing maternal identity and reducing people to markers of lineage. Such practices undermine individuality and obscure personal achievements.

By omitting last names in this story, I hope to remind readers of a time and a possibility when people were defined by their choices, actions, and identities rather than by their ancestry or affiliations.

Thank you for journeying with me into a world where names are simply names and individuality matters most.

Warm regards,
A. S. RAJANGAM

THE STORY BEGINS

Anu was exhausted. Not just from the sleepless nights of the past few days, but from the pervasive injustice and corruption engulfing his society. He was disheartened by how people had accepted this decay as the new normal, and he was frustrated with the newspaper where he worked, which chose to print stories about celebrity parties instead of addressing these pressing issues. His weariness had begun to seep into his health and spirit, dulling his once vibrant personality.

The doorbell rang, startling him. It was late, and he knew who it would be: his landlord, a kind woman in her early sixties. He hadn't paid his rent for the past two months, and the thought of facing her filled him with dread. For a moment, he considered staying silent, hoping she'd assume he wasn't home and leave. But his conscience wouldn't allow it. Against his will, he called out, "Coming!"

"Damn you, Mom," he muttered under his breath, cursing his mother for raising him to be so decent. He dragged himself to the door and opened it, bracing for the encounter.

Standing there, however, wasn't the older woman he expected, but someone who looked decades younger. His landlady, normally a slim, healthy woman with a few charming wrinkles, now appeared as if she were in her early twenties.

Anu blinked. For a moment, he wondered if the exhaustion was messing with his head. He tried to place her—maybe a niece? But the resemblance was uncanny. She had the same sharp eyes, the same confident posture. His thoughts drifted—should he flirt? But no, he hadn't paid rent in two months. The idea was ridiculous. Still, it was hard to ignore how strange it felt seeing her like this.

"I'm her granddaughter, Inara," she said, watching his expression carefully.

Anu nodded, though he was still trying to make sense of it. He stood there, stiff, the discomfort pressing in, but nothing came to mind. His mind flicked through possibilities but came up blank.

"Um, can I come in?" she asked.

"Yes, sure. Please, come in." He stepped aside to let her in, watching as she casually strolled into his living room, glancing around before settling on the couch.

"Though you're late on your rent, you keep your place quite clean," she remarked.

"Thank you," he replied awkwardly. "Can I offer you something? Coffee?"

She glanced toward the kitchen, where dirty dishes were piled in the sink, and smiled. "Looks like I spoke too soon."

He blushed, managing only a sheepish grin in response.

"Maybe later," she said, easing the tension. She gestured to a chair near the couch, inviting him to sit.

"I'm sorry. Please tell your grandma I'll pay the rent by next month. I quit my job a few months ago, and things have been tough," Anu explained as he sat down.

"Yes, I know. You quit four months ago because your ideals didn't align with the newspaper's direction. Blah, blah, blah. I know all about it," Inara said, her response catching him off guard. Anu was not just surprised but utterly shocked at how much she knew about him.

"I'm not here about the rent. I'm here to discuss something else," Inara continued.

Anu was completely confused now. What could she possibly want to talk to him about?

"Yes, please. What do you want to talk about?" he asked, trying to gather his wits.

She took a couple of cigarettes from a pack on the table and offered him one. He accepted it, still puzzled. She lit hers and passed him the lighter.

"I'm not her granddaughter. I am her," she said, exhaling a plume of smoke.

Anu froze, cigarette halfway to his lips. For a moment, he wondered if he had heard her wrong. But as he stared, something shifted. The corners of her eyes creased, faint lines appeared around her mouth, and then, just as quickly, they smoothed out again.

He didn't know what to say. His first instinct was to question it, but the words wouldn't form. Inara was watching him, amused by his confusion, as if she'd seen this reaction a hundred times before. She took another drag, as if it were the most natural thing in the world.

"How did you—" Anu started but stopped himself. The more he tried to make sense of it, the less sense it made.

Inara smiled, the same knowing smile that both unsettled and intrigued him. "Let me tell you a story," she said. She flicked the ash from her cigarette and looked toward the kitchen. "And how about that coffee now?"

PeTiTe

01 LUST

An overwhelming desire or craving, often for sexual pleasure, leading to actions that objectify others and prioritize physical gratification over emotional connections and respect for oneself and others.

At first, Austin thought it was just thunder. He rolled over in bed, trying to ignore the noise and drift back to sleep. It had been nearly six months since his confinement began. His crime? Nothing too severe—just running an independent laboratory and conducting biological research. Admittedly, some of his experiments had pushed ethical boundaries, resulting in a hefty penalty: a fine of one million and a year of house arrest.

The fine was trivial to him. After all, his home was a sixteenth-century manor, tucked away in the middle of nowhere. He hadn't been born into wealth but had earned billions through medical research. Despite his fortune, Austin was a lonely man, largely due to his unpleasant personality. He embodied many of the qualities people detest: arrogance, narcissism, and self-absorption. He had never understood romance, and during his tenure as a professor, he had coerced many of the women he deemed "doable" into "entertaining" him. But for the last six months, cut off from the outside world—and with none of those women wanting anything to do with him—he had been left with no other option than to satisfy himself.

In a strange way, Austin was grateful for the isolation. It had saved him from the pandemic ravaging the world. The disease was puzzling in its simplicity—its sole symptom was a severe headache, followed by vivid hallucinations. Yet it had a deadly edge. The brain, overwhelmed by the hallucinations, would eventually trigger bleeding from the body's openings, leading to death. Strangely, any scientist who dedicated time to studying the cause of the pandemic faced the same symptoms, ultimately meeting a definitive and untimely death.

Austin listened more carefully. The banging wasn't coming from outside; it echoed through the foyer, loud yet faltering, as though whoever was knocking was pausing between attempts to gather their strength.

Unable to sleep and growing curious about who would be knocking at his door at such an hour, especially in this dreadful weather, Austin dragged himself out of bed. Adjusting his robe, he made his way to the door.

When Austin opened the door, he was met by an unexpected sight: a young woman, perhaps in her late twenties, standing on his doorstep in the pouring rain. For a split second, he wondered if she was real or if his isolation had finally begun to play tricks on him. His gaze drifted to her muddy, ankle-length trekking boots, the rain steadily washing away the dirt. Above them, her jeans, torn in several places, gave her an unpolished, rugged look that seemed to suit her.

His gaze shifted upward to her vest, soaked through by the relentless downpour. The damp fabric clung to her frame, highlighting her toned build in a way that was noticeable yet unassuming. Just above her jeans, the vest left a small space, subtly hinting at the lean lines of her waist. The constant beat of the rain against the manor added to the surreal quality of her presence, and the wet fabric added a raw, unfiltered quality to her presence that stirred an unusual curiosity in him.

Finally, his eyes moved to her face, where her wet hair framed sharp, striking features. The rain had softened her appearance, yet she held an undeniable presence that made him pause. Though fresh blood stains marked her vest, he barely registered them, too absorbed in the unexpected allure of her arrival on this stormy night.

The rain was relentless, and even at the doorstep, the heavy downpour was drifting inside, still wetting her. With each quick, deep inhale she took, Austin felt his own breath hitch, losing more composure by the second. He stood there, mesmerized, oblivious to the rainwater pooling in the foyer.

More importantly, he ignored the bloodied man she was struggling to keep upright.

"Help us," she said in a thick Russian accent.

Austin's mind raced. He had always harbored a particular weakness for Russian women. It felt as though some divine force had shaped all his fantasies into this one perfect being and delivered her to his doorstep on a stormy night.

"If there's a flash of lightning behind her, this would be perfect," he thought, almost giddy with anticipation.

As if on cue, a brilliant streak of lightning lit up the sky behind her. Austin's heart raced. "The gods are smiling on me tonight," he thought, barely able to contain his excitement.

He quickly snapped back to the present, trying to compose himself. "Of course. Come in," he said, his focus still on her, hardly glancing at the man as he stepped forward to help her bring the injured man inside.

Once they were fully in the foyer, Austin closed the door, shutting out the storm.

"Please help us. This is my boyfriend, Anton. He's badly hurt," she pleaded, her voice urgent as she directed his attention to the bloodied man.

The bloodied man, Anton, weakly waved at Austin and tried to say something. But it looked like he hurt his throat and could hardly speak. Austin quickly examined him from afar, noticing that Anton had scratches all over his body, as if he had fallen from a hilltop, probably from the one near his manor. Anton was clutching the right side of his stomach tightly with his left hand, and there was a considerable amount of blood soaking through his clothing. A puncture wound, perhaps.

"What happened?" Austin asked.

"Well, we were hiking nearby…" She started stammering, "and it got dark and we felt lost in the forest… the forest on the hill… near here…" She paused to catch her breath.

Seeing her struggling to speak, Austin fetched a jar of water and a couple of glasses from a nearby table. He poured water into the glasses and handed one to her. She grabbed it quickly and drank it down. When finished, she took the other glass from Austin and tried to help Anton drink. He managed to swallow a little, though most of it spilled from his mouth.

After she finished helping Anton, she looked at Austin and continued, "I'm Ivanna. While we were up in the hills, we saw three men killing a fourth man. I screamed. They tried to kill us too. We ran, and we slipped down the hill."

Though her explanation was halting, Austin pieced together the gist of the story, knowing the terrain around his estate. Gently, he lifted Anton's hand from his stomach. Blood immediately welled up.

"He's been shot!" Austin exclaimed.

Ivanna nodded weakly, tears streaming down her face.

Austin quickly rushed inside and returned with several towels. He wrapped one around Anton's waist as tightly as he could to stem the bleeding. Anton lay on the floor, his arms limp, barely conscious.

Austin handed a towel to Ivanna, signaling for her to dry herself, and began gently drying Anton with another towel.

"We need to call the police. This is complicated, especially given my situation." He pointed to his ankle monitor.

Ivanna's eyes widened in shock, and she gave him a questioning look.

"I'm not a murderer, or anything dangerous" Austin reassured her. "It's just an ethical offense."

Ivanna, though confused, seemed somewhat relieved.

After all, she had no other choice.

"No. Not the police. Please!" she begged.

"Why not? He needs immediate medical attention, or he'll die. We should call an ambulance, and also I'll be in serious trouble if I don't call the police." Austin tried to make her understand the urgency.

"Please, don't ask me why. We can't call the police. Please, please!" Ivanna pleaded, tears flowing again.

Austin paced the room, deep in thought. He walked over to the bar in the adjacent study, still able to see Ivanna and Anton from where he stood. He poured himself a whiskey, and took a sip.

The manor was silent except for the faint rumble of distant thunder and Ivanna's soft, rhythmic sobbing.

Without a word, Austin knelt beside Anton and checked the wound again. Anton groaned in pain. The bleeding had slowed, likely because he'd already lost so much blood.

"He doesn't have long," Austin said matter-of-factly. "Maybe two, three hours before he dies from hemorrhaging." He paused, then added, "But… maybe I can help."

Ivanna lifted her head, her face a mix of confusion and hope.

"I have a laboratory downstairs... one I'm technically not supposed to use. But I could operate on him there, patch him up. I even have blood for a transfusion." Austin's lips curved into a faint smile, though his eyes betrayed a hint of uncertainty. "So, yes, I could save him."

Ivanna quickly stood up, her hope rekindled. "You can do that?" she asked, her voice trembling.

"Yes," Austin replied, his smile growing. "But I need your help to save him." He looked her in the eyes, letting the words hang in the air.

"Sure. Anything. Just tell me what to do," Ivanna said eagerly, wiping away her tears.

Austin's gaze softened, his words carefully measured. "I've been in isolation for six months," he said quietly. "I want company, closeness—someone to be with for a while."

Ivanna stiffened, the meaning of his words sinking in. Her

breath caught, and she quickly looked away, a flicker of panic crossing her face. She glanced toward Anton, lying motionless on the floor, then back at Austin, searching his face for any sign of compassion.

"My conditions are simple," he continued, his voice calm but unyielding. "Just one hour of your time—no force, no demands beyond a little connection. After that, I'll do everything I can to save him. He has only a few hours left, and every moment counts."

Ivanna's hands trembled, gripping the soaked fabric of her vest tightly as she struggled to steady herself. The enormity of his request weighed heavily on her. She wanted to scream, to push him away, but desperation held her back. Her gaze shifted between Austin and Anton, trapped in an impossible choice.

Austin seemed to notice her struggle, his gaze steady but unreadable. "You're always free to say no or to call for an ambulance. I won't stop you. But know, I may be his best chance right now."

Ivanna met his eyes, her expression one of silent, anguished defiance, but she said nothing, the weight of the decision pressing down as she wrestled with herself.

02 DILIGENCE

Committing to hard work, perseverance, and a strong work ethic, consistently striving to fulfill one's duties and responsibilities, and approaching tasks with a positive and determined attitude, leading to personal growth and achievement.

It was a beautiful sunny day, neither too hot nor too cold, with a perfect twenty-two degrees and a gentle breeze, making it ideal for lunch outside.

The campus was unusually empty due to the Independence Day holiday, with only a few international students left behind. Alejandro, with his food in hand, was waiting for Inara to join him.

"My food is getting cold," he muttered to himself in his smooth Mexican accent as he unwrapped his burrito.

"Sorry to keep you waiting! There weren't many options for a vegetarian," Inara apologized, squeezing into the narrow space between the table and the bench.

Though beautiful, Inara felt insecure about her size. She was what some might call "curvy" in a world where body-shaming was common but indirect. Just a few months ago, a professor had shamed her, affecting her deeply. Since then, she had isolated herself from everyone except

Alejandro and her boyfriend, Abraham, and focused on intense workouts and innovative research.

Coincidentally, Abraham, also a fellow student from India, had chosen the worst time to confess his feelings for her—the same evening she was shamed by the professor. With her self-esteem shattered, she believed he was playing a cruel joke on her, especially considering his super attractive, petite Chinese friend, Irene; she couldn't fathom why Abraham would be interested in her, a self-perceived 'fat' Indian girl.

"I've always been drawn to your intelligence," Abraham told her, unaware of what she had gone through earlier that day. "Your body never defined my feelings for you, but that doesn't mean I'm not physically attracted to you, because I am."

On any other day, Inara would have been ecstatic, but the professor's cruel words still echoed in her mind. Her confidence was at rock bottom, her self-doubt at an all-time high. Poor Abraham didn't know and later regretted choosing that day to confess.

"Did you look at the structural problem we have for the Hyperloop?" Alejandro asked, ignoring her apology and not caring if she ate her salad.

Inara, in the middle of dressing her salad, looked up and shrugged. "Not yet. I've been busy."

Alejandro sighed. "I've been thinking about how to optimize the design. There's a lot of similarity between the Hyperloop fuselage and an aircraft fuselage. Both deal with significant pressure differences. The design optimization algorithm could work for both industries, right?"

Inara nodded, considering his words. "That's true. But why stop at aircraft applications? Why not use it for high-pressure containers or submarines too? Expand our market?"

"Well, compression and expansion work differently in design consideration. Also, weight savings are crucial in aerospace and Hyperloop applications. Other industries don't prioritize it as much. Submarines are primarily defense-related, and we're too early with our network to get into that market. I believe the market for our design optimization algorithm is here in aerospace and Hyperloop," Alejandro countered.

Inara thought for a moment, then said, "I've actually been working on integrating a design optimization algorithm with a computational model for overall aircraft design. Given that Hyperloop is still developing, and I personally don't think it will ever be successful, I kind of put the work on it on hold. My new design optimization algorithm just requires inputs like seat capacity, range, category, etc., for an aircraft and the AI tries various cabin layouts, builds the fuselage, and designs the plane considering structural and aerodynamic limits. It's developed around quantum computing, so preliminary designs are ready in four hours. A detailed, optimized design takes about twenty-four hours."

Alejandro, listening intently, took a slow bite of his burrito and closed his eyes for a moment.

"And I've integrated quantum AI, which also considers intellectual property rights versus design freedom, optimizing accordingly," Inara continued in her calm tone.

"That's amazing. Why didn't you tell me earlier?" Alejandro's voice rose in a mix of frustration and surprise, startling Inara. She couldn't place whether he was angry, excited, or just exasperated with her. "Where do you think I've been these last few days? I met with the CEO of AeroBridge yesterday. If I'd known, I could have presented something substantial instead of going empty-handed and wasting the opportunity."

Inara did her best not to cry, realizing he was angry and she might have made their company lose a business opportunity. "I wanted to give you a working tool as a birthday gift. Sorry. And happy birthday?"

Her attempt at a puppy face, tears brimming in her eyes, seemed to work in softening Alejandro's anger.

"Well, it's your birthday today too, isn't it?" he asked, his tone softening with a touch of shared amusement.

She nodded softly, eyes closed, trying to hide her tears.

"Then let's celebrate," Alejandro said, reaching into his bag and pulling out a couple of expensive chocolate bars. He made a V-shape with them, placing his face in between the V, smiling at Inara.

Inara looked confused as Alejandro continued his grin, repeatedly raising his eyebrows.

He handed one of the chocolate bars to Inara. She, still puzzled, accepted hers, looking at him for an explanation.

"I knew about your plans for the project—and the birthday surprise," Alejandro said with a grin. "Well, Abraham blurted it out to me a few weeks ago when we met at the gym. It's not his fault; he just assumed I knew. Anyway, I didn't want to spoil your surprise, but I also didn't want to miss the opportunity with AeroBridge."

Inara's eyes widened in disbelief. "So, you knew?"

"Yes, and we secured a ten-million-dollar investment to demonstrate the prototype," Alejandro announced.

Inara blinked, a quick shock washing over her before excitement took hold. She looked relieved and happy, hardly able to believe the news.

"Ten million, and I get only this chocolate?" she asked, raising an eyebrow playfully.

Alejandro laughed. "Well, it's still just on paper. Once we receive the funding, we'll each get a million as founders. The rest? That goes into the company—for further developments, research, hiring… the works."

Inara said nothing, but her expression shifted, a quiet determination settling in. She glanced at the chocolate, then back at Alejandro, giving a slow nod, as if acknowledging the start of something much bigger.

Alejandro's grin widened. "We're millionaires now, Inara. No more one meal a day or cheap food!" he exclaimed, the excitement finally breaking through.

But Inara had much higher ambitions. Ten million was just the beginning for her. She shared in Alejandro's joy but soon composed herself. They quickly shifted to discussing the investment details, AeroBridge's expectations, and the project timelines—all while Inara calmly nibbled on her salad and Alejandro took slow bites of his burrito.

"This is a good first million," Alejandro commented. After taking a deep breath and looking at his half-eaten burrito, he added, "I'm not hungry anymore. You?"

"I want more. One million isn't enough. I want to make billions… maybe even trillions," Inara said, her voice soft but resolute. She stared down at her salad, unaware that Alejandro's comment was only about the burrito.

Her determined voice surprised Alejandro—pleasantly, yet with an underlying sense of unease. He admired Inara's ambition deeply, but as he unwrapped his chocolate and ate in silence, a quiet doubt crept in. He wondered if he could truly keep pace with her relentless ambition.

After a few moments, Inara broke the silence, "Did you listen to Abraham and Irene's presentation on quantum-DNA?"

"Yes, but vaguely. I was at the airport and could barely listen to their presentation. Is it any good?" Alejandro asked.

"It might seem like a fantasy, but there's strong potential. Abraham and Irene are nerds, but they don't talk nonsense," Inara assured him. "Should I explain, or did you get the idea of quantum DNA?"

"I got the gist—manipulating material properties at the quantum level to change how it behaves. Am I right, or was it something else?" Alejandro asked, wanting to ensure they were on the same page.

"Yes, that's right. Now, imagine creating a super material by manipulating its properties at the quantum level. A thread so strong it could carry a truck, a fabric resistant to extreme heat and flames, or material that could withstand bullets. The applications are endless." She paused, looking directly at Alejandro. "We could focus our next business plan on that since we already have the prototype for AeroBridge ready. What do you think?"

03 CHARITY

Demonstrating love, generosity, and selflessness by giving to those in need, showing compassion, and performing acts of kindness without expecting anything in return, thereby fostering community and alleviating suffering.

"When you develop yourself to the point where your belief in yourself is so strong that you know you can accomplish anything you put your mind to, your future will be unlimited."

The host of the online video streaming channel began her show with an inspirational quote, pausing for dramatic effect. "Today, I'll talk about qAI, a startup by two students who secured millions in investment before graduating—and now, billions. What did they do to make leading aerospace companies like AeroBridge invest in them? A revolutionary design optimization software, incorporating advanced AI and quantum computing, saving hundreds of thousands of hours in development. But is that all they do, or is there more? The CEO and co-founder of qAI, Alejandro, is with us today to tell us more about qAI and their innovations."

The camera zoomed out and panned to reveal Alejandro sitting next to the host.

"First things first, leading television channels are eager to host you but haven't succeeded. Yet, you chose to accept my invitation. Why?" the host asked, as the camera focused on Alejandro.

"I was a student not long ago. Though I come from a financially stable family, I chose not to take their support. My friend and I struggled to afford even one good meal a day. We had to save for a decent drink once a month and couldn't think about vacations. There was even fear in asking a girl out, knowing I couldn't afford even a coffee if she said yes. So, I know this can help students like you more than corporate-driven television channels."

Alejandro was happy to answer this previously agreed-upon question, showing the world that he is not just a rich kid but someone who went through struggles to attain his success.

"That sounds noble of you," the host praised Alejandro. "Yet the software you developed made you a multi-millionaire, while thousands lost their jobs. How do you feel about that?" The host seized the opportunity to challenge her guest.

Alejandro had anticipated such criticism but hadn't expected it come this early in his first interview.

"It's true that around five thousand lost their jobs in AeroBridge. But not all of them are jobless. Almost three thousand now work for qAI because they possessed the necessary competence for our other projects. Some fifteen hundred were sponsored by qAI to develop their skills in areas they chose to find other jobs. Finally, we supported some five hundred close to retirement by hiring them as consultants. Their experience and wisdom are invaluable. Some insights they have can't be obtained from any literature. No AI can make suggestions like they do just by looking at the data. Their intuition made me believe that machines can never take over humanity." He paused briefly, his tone steady, the weight of responsibility evident in his eyes.

Alejandro, composed but unyielding, met the host's gaze with a measured calm that carried an unspoken message: there were boundaries, and she had just crossed one. His presence conveyed a silent challenge, urging her to reconsider her choice of questions.

"That is… how should I say… ummmm…" The host, sensing the firmness in Alejandro's gaze, offered a nervous smile and quickly pivoted. "You're, uh, truly noble," she added, with a forced cheeriness. Clearly attempting to smooth things over, she continued, "Now, let's talk about your latest venture—a billion-dollar investment in such a young startup. It's unheard of! What could possibly be so revolutionary?"

"Teleportation!" Alejandro chuckled.

The host looked puzzled, raising an eyebrow for Alejandro to clarify.

"What do you mean by teleportation? The art of disappearing from one place and appearing in another like magicians do?" the host asked, hoping for a more detailed explanation.

"Yes!" Alejandro replied with a straight face. "But not humans in our case. At least, not yet. This little box, we call it the PeTiTe," he explained, taking a device out of the duffle bag he brought with him, "can teleport any non-organic matter up to a mass of one thousand grams to anywhere a counterpart is located."

The PeTiTe looked like a small weighing machine with a spherical cage-like arrangement on the top.

"What does it do? How does it work?" the impatient host asked.

"Wait. Let me show you." Alejandro took out another similar device from the bag and placed it at the other end of the table. "Can I have your bracelet?"

"I hope I get it back. It's a gift from my boyfriend," the host replied, slightly wary.

"Of course!" Alejandro assured as he took the bracelet and placed it in the spherical cage of the first device. Then he used his smartphone to do something. "Watch closely. Don't blink! For when you blink, you'll miss it." He continued with a flourish, "In three… two… ONE!!!"

The bracelet vanished from the first device and reappeared on the second one.

The host was speechless, her eyes wide in disbelief.

"It's no magic, but science," Alejandro said, as if reading her thoughts. "Yes, teleportation is possible now through science."

"Wow!" the host exclaimed. "This is some serious sci-fi superhero stuff. But how? What's the technology behind it?"

"Quantum DNA," Alejandro explained, "a topic ignored by many as fantasy or interesting to only a few."

"Dear viewers, to know more about what quantum DNA is, please refer to my video on the same, available on my channel under the title 'Quantum DNA: A Scientific Breakthrough or a Failed Fantasy,' where I discussed the publications by Abraham and Irene, the inventors of the concept," the host interjected, to let the audience know that they can always learn more about quantum DNA on her channel.

"You are the only person who has not worked on the topic but spoke about it. I watched your video, and you explained the concept quite well. Better than the scientists who invented it. Believe me, I was there. I strongly recommend viewers watch the video to understand what quantum DNA is." Alejandro promoted the host's channel.

The host's cheeks reddened with pride. "But can you explain how your device works? Maybe in simpler terms so non-science enthusiasts can understand too?"

"What is quantum DNA—or simply, qDNA?" Alejandro began, leaning back in his chair with a hint of a smile. "Think of it as a kind of code or memory embedded within each atom at the quantum level. Just like DNA holds information about a living being, qDNA contains essential details about each atom—what it is, where it belongs, its purpose, and its relationship to other atoms around it. All this information is stored on a microscopic level, within each atom's very structure."

He continued, "Now, while the host covered the basic idea of qDNA earlier, what's unique to us is how we've used it to achieve teleportation. You see, qDNA includes spatial information—where each atom 'thinks' it exists. We figured out how to read that location data and then tell the atom it's somewhere else entirely. In other words, we're redirecting its memory of where it belongs."

"But the energy requirement?" The host raised an eyebrow. "I believe it's similar to creating a wormhole. Several have tried, but the energy required is enormous. Yet your device looks like it's using one or two triple-A batteries. How is that possible?"

"Ha. Ha. Ha." Alejandro chuckled. "The batteries we use are for the electronics in the PeTiTe. For teleportation, the atoms use the energy within and around them. In spiritual terms, it uses the energy of the universe." He laughed again.

"Ha. Ha. Ha." The host joined in. "Sounds like finally science is explaining religion."

"Yes!" Alejandro replied, his tone serious. "It's all about faith. You know the phrase 'with every fiber of your being'? It means that when belief is strong enough, the impossible can become possible. This may sound religious and total nonsense to a scientist, but it's the basis for our invention. We're limited only by our imagination. Imagine someone with the ability to teleport—they do so by visualizing a location so vividly that every atom in their body believes it's already there. They would alter spatial information at the qDNA level, and their body would transport them there, retaining all other essential data. There are terabytes of information stored in each atom that we haven't decoded yet. Once we do, anything will become possible."

Alejandro paused, realizing he had given a lot of information and decided to take a break.

"Are you saying a person with self-healing powers is possible?" The host, still excited, asked. "That would be incredible. I've always wanted to see someone with that kind of ability in real life."

"Of course!" Alejandro continued with enthusiasm. "It's all about the ability of atoms to retain memory and resist external influences. When part of the memory strongly refuses to change due to external factors, it retains its properties. For example, making plastic behave like steel or changing water to gasoline. This could actually solve our fossil fuel problem and many other."

"That sounds amazing. What happened to that?" the host inquired.

"Well, while exploring that part of qDNA, we stumbled upon information related to space—not just what it is, but where it is," Alejandro began, leaning slightly forward as if drawing the host in with a secret. "Each atom defines its location relative to others. When we altered the spatial information for one atom, the rest followed because of their interdependency. That's how we achieved teleportation with minimal energy."

He paused for a moment, letting the concept settle, then continued with a slight smile. "Now, changing the properties of a material—like turning water into gasoline—is far more complex. It requires altering the fundamental structure of the atoms themselves." Alejandro gestured subtly with his hands, emphasizing the complexity of such a task. "But spatial information? That's simpler—it's often the same for different materials. Moving an object is far easier than altering what it fundamentally is."

Alejandro shifted in his seat, the weight of the next statement clear on his face. "This discovery—changing the properties of materials—is going to challenge everything we know about physics. The laws of conservation of energy and mass might no longer apply." He looked up at the host for a brief moment before continuing, his voice carrying an almost playful tone. "Imagine turning air into a rose for a magic trick, or transforming cancer cells into healthy ones with a simple touch. Maybe Jesus was a mutant who knew how to alter memory at a quantum level."

"You know, that's a headline waiting to happen!" The host smiled. "One last question before we end this segment. Can you tell us what PeTiTe stands for?"

Alejandro grinned. "It stands for Personal Time Travel and Teleportation."

The host's eyes widened. "Time travel? Are you serious? When are you going to change everything—our entire understanding of the universe!"

Alejandro chuckled softly. "Not yet. We're focusing on teleportation for now. Time travel is still theoretical, but who knows what the future holds?"

The host, still intrigued, concluded, "Thank you so much for your time, Alejandro. This has been enlightening, and I'm sure our viewers are as amazed as I am. We look forward to seeing how qAI will change the world."

"Thank you for having me," Alejandro said with a smile.

The host turned to the camera, smiling. "Stay tuned for more incredible stories of innovation and inspiration. See you next time!"

LUCK

Adrien and Andre sat at their usual corner table in a modest tea shop, sipping steaming cups of chai. The shop, with its faded walls and rickety furniture, was nestled in a lower-middle-class neighborhood of Goa, far from the opulence of tourist hotspots. The air was thick with the scent of spices, and the low hum of casual chatter filled the room.

Adrien, lean and tall with delicate fingers, casually draped his arm around Andre's shoulder. His French accent was barely audible over the clinking of cups and murmur of conversations. Beside him, Andre, slightly shorter but well-built, rested his head against Adrien's arm, his Filipino features softened by a warm smile.

They weren't just two tourists enjoying chai; their presence here was part of a carefully orchestrated mission. Adrien and Andre were operatives for the International Security Agency, known as ISA. Their colleagues called them 'The Lions'—a nod to their fierce unity, like a lion's pride, both strong and exclusive. The name was also a subtle tribute to their relationship, linking 'pride' to their bond as a gay couple and the strength of their close-knit team, known for its loyalty and the difficulty of gaining entry.

Across the street, on the first floor of a nondescript house, a room had become the focal point of their surveillance. The agency had identified this location as a key node in a terrorist plot. Adrien and Andre had been tracking the suspects for weeks, believing that the individuals renting the room were planning a major attack in India.

As they flirted and whispered softly to each other, their eyes occasionally darted towards the room. Their chemistry was palpable—a silent dance of glances and subtle shifts signaling when to watch and when to relax. They had perfected this routine over years together, seamlessly blending personal affection with professional duty.

Andre leaned closer, his breath warm against Adrien's ear.

"You know, for a place so simple, it's actually quite charming," he murmured, his eyes flickering towards the window of the room they were monitoring.

Adrien smiled, his gaze shifting to Andre before returning to the window. "Charming in a 'we could be doing this anywhere else' kind of way?" he teased, a playful glint in his eye.

"No, quite the opposite. Over the past month here, we've maybe spent around a thousand. Imagine a similar vacation in a remote beach town in France—we'd have spent at least ten times that." Andre used air quotes around "vacations" to indicate Adrien what he mean by it.

"Well, remember the resource utilization map we saw at the natural museum during our holiday in Vienna? It said we'd need two and a half Earths if everyone lived like the French. But we'd only need sixty percent of Earth's resources if we lived like Indians," Adrien added thoughtfully. "How is it in the Philippines?"

"It used to be like this—simple. But lately, things have changed drastically. More Westernization, more capitalism. I hardly recognize my village these days. There's even a KFC there now."

"I bet a lot has changed in India too. It's such a huge country, so you don't notice it much in remote places like this. But in cities and even smaller towns, I'm sure the changes have been drastic," Adrien said, trying to make Andre feel better about his own country's shifts.

"True. India has a lot of bright minds and technological advancements compared to us. Look at how many satellites they've launched," Andre replied.

"Oh, that reminds me of a question I've had for a while. You're the technical one, so maybe you can answer it," Adrien said, giving Andre a gentle nudge to steer him away from his thoughts about the changes back home.

Andre looked at him, taking a sip of his tea, waiting for him to continue.

"We're launching so many satellites, which means we're sending a lot of materials away from Earth. Doesn't that make us lighter? Couldn't that affect the balance of the universe, or at least mess with the Earth's relationship with the moon or something?"

A random man in a striped vest and a lungi, who looked like he'd just rolled out of bed and came straight to the shop for his morning coffee, was clearly eavesdropping on their conversation. He glanced at Andre, as if eager to hear the answer.

Andre noticed him but didn't mind; it might actually help their mission if they could blend in with the locals. "Are you asking if losing weight would decrease the gravitational pull between Earth and the moon, making the moon drift away?" Andre asked.

Adrien grinned and nodded, as did the random man.

"And by the same logic, would the reduced weight cause Earth to move away from the Sun, getting colder?"

Again, Adrien and the random man nodded.

"Let me give you some numbers. Each rocket we launch weighs about a thousand tons—roughly a million kilograms, okay?"

They nodded, following his explanation.

"We've launched around ten thousand rockets so far."

"Actually, closer to fifteen thousand," the random man corrected.

Andre, surprised, continued with a newfound respect for the man. "Let's exaggerate and say it's thirty thousand launches. That's thirty thousand times one million kilograms, which is…"

"Thirty billion," the man said, hesitantly but correctly.

"Yes, exactly," Andre acknowledged. "Now consider this: the mass of the Earth is something close to six followed by twenty-four zeros. Losing thirty billion kilograms is like me losing the very tip of one of my hairs," he said, pulling out a strand from his forearm to illustrate the minuscule change.

"Ah!" Adrien and the random man exclaimed together.

"Here's the interesting part: we actually keep ninety-nine percent of the rocket mass within the atmosphere. The fuel turns into gas, parts fall back to Earth, and only a small fraction orbits as satellites. Even that weight, still in orbit, is considered part of Earth's mass."

"What? That's crazy. Why all the numbers then?" Adrien pretended to be annoyed and playfully punched Andre's shoulder. Andre raised his arms and dodged the mock punches, laughing.

Their banter was abruptly cut short by a blinding flash from the room across the street. The blinding flash hit like a thunderclap, followed instantly by the deafening roar of the explosion. The shockwave tore through the street, shattering windows and sending clouds of dust and debris billowing into the air. The tea cups rattled violently on their table, chai sloshing over the sides as the floor trembled beneath them.

The blast jolted them both. They exchanged a glance filled with shock and confusion, silently questioning whether the terrorists had made a mistake while assembling the bomb.

04 PRIDE

An excessive belief in one's own abilities, worth, or importance, often resulting in arrogance, a lack of humility, and a disdain for others, leading to a separation from community and the inability to recognize one's flaws.

The time is 7:38 PM. There is still natural light outside, but Abraham has chosen to close all the blinds. He turns on the lights and sits on his couch, with the tablet positioned in front of him. He opens the camera app to check if the lighting is good, ensuring his dark-skinned face is clearly visible against the white wall background.

"Should I turn that light on as well?" he thought to himself. "I still have seven more minutes before the call, but I'm comfortably placed."

Despite his comfort, Abraham decides to get up and turn on the lamp for better lighting. He doesn't want any distractions during the call.

As he stood by the tall lamp, the glow reminded him of that afternoon in the park, months ago, when he and Inara sat beneath a tree. This particular conversation happened a few months after they started dating. He wouldn't have brought it up if Inara hadn't been so intensely focused on reducing her size. It was clear she was not just determined but obsessed with getting slim.

They were sitting under a tree in a park at that time, with Inara resting the back of her head on his chest and reading her book, Integration of AI and Quantum Computing, while enjoying Abraham's embrace around her waist from behind. As she read, her whole body seemed to respond, her fingers trembling lightly against the pages—petite signs of her mind working, of her absorbing the complexity of quantum computing integrating with artificial intelligence with every fiber of her being.

Noticing the subtle tremor in her hand, Abraham gently took it in his, offering silent support as her body shivered under the weight of what she was learning. But a part of him assumed it might have been due to her rigorous workout routine earlier that day. Perhaps, he thought, she was pushing herself too hard, and the exhaustion was now settling in.

After a moment, Inara closed the book and her eyes, leaning fully into Abraham's embrace. She took a deep breath, needing the pause to allow her mind and body to fully absorb it—a small break to let the knowledge settle deeply within her.

"You know there's a big difference between determination and obsession?" Abraham said softly, his voice calm, still thinking she might be overexerting herself.

Inara quietly set the book aside, releasing herself from that sweet embrace, which was no longer sweet, and positioned herself in front of him, staring deep into his eyes. Abraham felt confused. Like many men, he wasn't sure what he had said wrong, but he knew he had said something he shouldn't have. He could feel his heart beating faster in the silence and his prefrontal cortex judging him.

"What I meant is, you see..." he stammered, trying to find the right words. "You wanting to slim down is fine, but at what cost?"

Realizing that continuing to talk might not help, he chose awkward silence.

"No, no. Go on!" Inara straightened her back. "Please,

finish what you were trying to tell me."

Abraham felt completely trapped. He realized he had to be very careful with his next words. He needed to fine-tune his verbal, physical, and emotional communication so that she would understand that what he said and was going to say was with good intention, and not make her angry. He tried to recall everything his friends had taught him about girls, the books he had read, but his mind drew a blank.

A bead of sweat popped out on his forehead and started rolling down his cheek.

"I'm not telling you not to exercise. But I think you're pushing yourself more than your body can take," he said, taking a deep breath.

"But that's how power exercise works. It pushes your limits," she responded calmly, without taking her eyes off him.

"Yes, I agree," Abraham replied immediately. "But first, you should stay within your limits for a while and then push them up gradually."

Inara let out a soft, almost hollow chuckle, her gaze still fixed on him. "It's funny you think I don't know that."

Abraham felt trapped again. He couldn't think of a response that wouldn't look like he actually thought that yet still convey his point.

"I don't think that," he said with a smile, knowing that neither she nor he believed it. "But what I want to say is that there's nothing wrong with taking a break and relaxing a bit."

Inara's internal frustration was palpable as Abraham spoke. She had already heard similar reassurances before, and now they seemed to only deepen her sense of being misunderstood.

Her feelings of frustration were complex, stemming from her struggle to convey that her efforts were not about conforming to others' expectations but about personal goals she couldn't easily explain.

She remained silent, hoping he would realize the gravity of the situation and give him a chance to recover from the damage he had caused in their relationship.

"See, you are the most brilliant and intelligent girl I have ever met," Abraham continued, oblivious to the damage he was continuing to cause. "You are beautiful as you are. Don't let the world's definition of beauty affect your self-confidence."

Inara's gaze lowered as she listened, feeling a mix of frustration and sadness. Abraham's words, though well-intentioned, seemed to miss the mark. She felt isolated, as if her struggles were being oversimplified by his reassurance.

She struggled to voice her real feelings, unable to convey how deeply misunderstood she felt. Her internal conflict grew as Abraham continued to speak, his words amplifying her sense of disconnection.

His memory faded back to the present as the hand he kept close to the lamp felt its heat.

He checked the time. It was only 7:40 PM. There were still five more minutes until the call. He sat back on the couch comfortably, his head on one armrest and his legs over the other.

His eyes felt tired from all the movies he had been watching over the past week. He closed his eyes to give them a rest. As his eyelids shut, the quiet around him pulled him back to that call a week ago. Inara's voice echoed in his mind, the words still lingering like unfinished business.

"We are two different people," she had said. "We are from different cultures, even though we are from the same country."

This time, he remembered to remain silent and didn't react to her words. He had been silent out of frustration. He could feel that she wasn't happy with the relationship in the past months. It all started when she, along with Alejandro, actively started their own company, qAI, and she was completely immersed in the projects. He felt like she spent more time developing the company and slimming down and not enough time with him. At that time, they were in a long-distance relationship as Abraham had moved back to his home country, India, for work. They used to talk for hours over the phone, but now there were days when they didn't even message each other.

"It's just the culture we grew up in. Once we are together, we'll adapt to each other and change," Abraham had said, though wanting to be silent, he didn't want to give up on their relationship.

"I just need time to think. Can you not contact me for the next week?" Inara had asked him.

Abraham felt hurt because she seemed to have ignored his offer.

"If that helps you, of course," Abraham had responded calmly, despite the frustration he felt within. "Next week at the same time? At 7:45. Call me?"

He waited for her confirmation. She nodded her head gently and hung up the call.

Abraham came back to the present. He checked his watch; it showed twenty seconds past 7:46. Frustration welled up inside him—Inara still hadn't called. Had she forgotten, or was she hesitating? He felt a pang of annoyance, thinking she might be waiting for him to make the first move. Maybe she assumed he would call her.

With that thought, Abraham decided to call her himself. As he turned on the tablet, ready to call her, a notification caught his eye. His heart skipped a beat. She had called. At 7:45, right on time. And he had missed it, too wrapped up in his memories to notice. His gut twisted with a sinking feeling as he immediately pressed to call her back.

Inara answered the call right away. She looked extremely tired, as if she hadn't slept the whole week. This gave Abraham some confidence that she had done serious thinking. He felt sad for her. He wished he could be right next to her, hug her, and tell her everything would be fine.

"How are you?" he asked. "You look tired."

She gave a faint smile.

"So, are you ready to talk now?" Abraham asked. "Did you get to think freely?"

She nodded calmly.

Abraham felt slightly frustrated because he felt like he was begging her to talk. "Well, go on. I'll listen."

"Yes, I was thinking about us this past week. You were there when I was low. You supported me and encouraged me when I needed it the most," Inara paused and continued. "But recently, I feel judged. It wasn't new to me, but when it came from you, it hurts."

"I'm sorry to make you feel that way. That was not my intention," Abraham interrupted but immediately realized he was breaking her flow. "Sorry, continue."

Inara took a few deep breaths while Abraham forgot to breathe, eagerly waiting for her to continue speaking.

"I know you speak your mind and are honest. I can understand that. But sometimes, I just want to rest on your chest and talk about my day, my work, my life without feeling judged. Without even feeling like I'm being judged. I just want you to listen. I know it's too much to ask. People don't change..."

"So, how do you want to do it?" Abraham interrupted again.

"Do what?" Inara asked, confused.

"This! This breakup. Isn't that what you're trying to do here? Last week, you said we are two different people, and today you're saying people don't change. So, isn't breaking up the natural next step?"

Inara remained silent. Disappointment hurt the core of her heart, and sadness blocked her from speaking. She focused all her strength on holding back her tears.

"Anyway, I won't disturb you anymore. Wish you all the best in your life!"

Abraham reached for his tablet and disconnected the call. The moment the screen went dark, the weight of his words hit him. He hadn't meant to end things this way—hadn't meant to sound so final. But now, it was done. He dropped his body on the couch, staring at the ceiling, his mind racing as if searching for some way to undo what had just happened. His frustration built, followed quickly by regret. He closed his eyes and tried not to think about it, crying gently out of anger—at her, at himself.

Inara's tears fell as she ended the call, her sobs filling the room, unseen and unheard by Abraham. Her hands clutched her face, and she struggled to contain the flood of emotions she had been holding back. Everything felt unresolved. The words she wanted to say—needed to say—still sat heavy in her chest, but now there was no one to hear them.

The clock on the tablet screen showed the time as 7:48 PM as the screen went dark.

05 ENVY

A feeling of discontent and resentment aroused by another's possessions, qualities, or luck, leading to a desire to possess what others have and often causing internal turmoil and strained relationships.

The ballroom of the ancient Chinese fort, with its carved wooden pillars and faded silk banners, stood as a relic of a bygone era. Once a space meant for fifty aristocrats, it now felt suffocating under the weight of modern excess. The room was crowded, filled with guests in tailored suits and designer gowns, all speaking loudly over the pounding beats from the DJ's modern setup.

The dim lighting from ancient lanterns, now fitted with electric bulbs, cast a strange, artificial glow over the room. The flickering lights highlighted the garish contrast between the old-world architecture and the overindulgent excess on display. Tables were piled with imported wine and extravagant dishes, a stark reminder of Governor Ayden's insatiable hunger for luxury—funded by the heavy taxes he imposed on the surrounding villages.

Ayden himself, draped in a suit that echoed imperial styles but tailored with a modern flair, moved through the crowd with calculated ease. His laughter boomed across the ballroom, cutting through the din of conversation as he paraded his wealth and influence to the provincial leaders gathered under his roof. Every interaction, every word, was designed to remind them of the power he held over their lives.

Ang, head of one of the few villages still outside Ayden's full control, was a stark contrast to the other leaders present. He wore simple clothing, reflecting his humble life and dedication to his people. Despite Ayden's influence and government connections, Ang had consistently resisted the governor's attempts to exploit his village, thanks in large part to his daughter Irene, who stood beside him that evening.

Irene was the first from her village to travel abroad for her education, where she earned a doctorate in quantum physics before returning home to dedicate her life to the village. She was admired by men, revered by women, and idolized by children—a quiet but persistent challenge to Ayden's authority. Her very existence reminded him of the limits to his reach, a fact that gnawed at him even as he smiled.

Ayden had tried before to bring them under his control, but Ang had always managed to sidestep direct confrontation. This time, however, Ayden was determined to provoke a response he could use against them. His lavish party wasn't just a celebration—it was a carefully orchestrated trap.

As the evening wore on, the guests became increasingly inebriated. Laughter turned coarse, with people stumbling over their gowns and polished shoes, their hands growing bolder with each drink. Clusters of men gathered near the bar, voices booming as they slurred taunts and raised their glasses in mock toasts to Ayden's "generosity." Some of the men began harassing the women, using their drunkenness as an excuse for inappropriate behavior. While some women recoiled and tried to distance themselves, others, seeing an opportunity to escape their harsh lives, played along with the attention. For them, enduring such advances seemed like the only way to improve their circumstances.

Irene and Ang positioned themselves near the edge of the

room, deliberately staying out of the main crowd. The dim light barely touched where they stood, casting them in shadow and creating a sense of separation from the chaos unfolding in the center of the ballroom. They exchanged only brief glances and a few quiet words, both preferring to observe rather than engage.

Irene's eyes swept over the room, taking in the drunken laughter and inappropriate behavior. Her expression remained neutral, but each passing moment deepened the quiet disgust she felt. Her father, by contrast, stood rooted, his calm smile masking his thoughts. Ang's confidence and wisdom were evident in his posture—he had faced ugliness before, but in their village, he had kept it at bay. It was only under Ayden's influence that such behavior had taken root in these parts.

Both of them knew this gathering had little to do with celebration. It was Ayden's way of reminding them of his power, a display meant to provoke and intimidate. Yet despite their silence, the bond between father and daughter was unmistakable. Together, they stood apart, their quiet dignity contrasting sharply with the debauchery unfolding around them.

Ayden, sensing the moment was right, plucked two drinks from a nearby table and swaggered toward them, his men trailing behind at a respectful distance. His approach was a performance, arms wide and voice boisterous, masking the menace beneath his exaggerated friendliness.

"Ang! How's my favorite village leader enjoying the party?" Ayden called out, a fake warmth in his tone. His grin stretched wide as he approached, but it was Irene his eyes latched onto, his gaze invasive.

Ang bowed slightly, his words measured. "Governor, it's hard to enjoy a party knowing my people are struggling to make ends meet."

Ayden barely registered the comment, his attention now fixed fully on Irene. His movements grew slower, more deliberate, as he positioned himself closer to her. Holding his drink just inches from her, the cold glass grazed against her skin, making her step back instinctively.

"Ah, Ang is still stuck in his old ways," Ayden smirked, swaying slightly, though it was hard to tell how much of his intoxication was real. His gaze lingered on Irene, a lecherous gleam in his eye. "But you, sweetie... surely you can find something to enjoy here?" He leaned in, using his drunkenness as an excuse to invade her space.

Irene tensed, her face hardening. "I agree with my father, Governor. And please, don't call me 'sweetie.'" Her tone was cold, but she kept it polite, holding onto the last shreds of formality.

Ayden's smirk deepened as he swayed closer, his breath reeking of alcohol. "What's wrong with 'sweetie'? What do the men you sleep with call you? Babe?" His eyes slid down to her neckline, lingering in a way that made her skin crawl.

Irene tried to step away, but Ayden's men had subtly blocked her in, closing off any escape routes. The wall behind her left her trapped.

Before Ang could intervene, another of Ayden's men intercepted him, making it clear he wasn't going anywhere. Ang, though calm, watched the scene with growing concern, his gaze darting anxiously toward his daughter.

Ayden, emboldened by her vulnerability, leaned in, his voice lowering to a taunting whisper. "You think those foreign men are better than me, huh? What could you possibly know without a taste of this?" He gestured at himself. "How about you tell me how I measure up in the morning?"

Irene's eyes flared with anger as Ayden grabbed her wrist, pulling her roughly toward him. She yanked herself free with a sharp jerk, her face twisting with disgust.

"Look at her, acting all pure," Ayden sneered to his men. "You know what we call girls like you, who stay late at parties dressed like that?" His voice dropped to a venomous whisper. "A bitch."

The word stung, but her response came quicker. Without hesitation, Irene swung her hand, the sharp crack of her slap cutting through the air. The entire room seemed to hold its breath as the sound echoed through the space, silencing the music and chatter. Partygoers froze in place, their eyes darting toward the source of the commotion.

As a ripple of disbelief spread through the crowd, some guests stared at Irene with a mixture of shock and admiration, while others shifted nervously, avoiding eye contact with either her or Ayden. A few women, standing toward the back, exchanged subtle glances of approval—savoring the brief moment of defiance in a room dominated by men like Ayden. But most of the men grumbled under their breath, clearly uneasy with the boldness of Irene's action. They exchanged cautious looks, reluctant to react openly, fearing Ayden's response.

The tension was thick, the atmosphere charged with unspoken words as the ballroom seemed to teeter on the edge of chaos.

Ayden stood stunned, his hand rising slowly to his cheek. But as Irene glared at him, breathless with fury, his lips curled into a twisted smile. He winked at her before turning and walking away, his hand still rubbing his cheek.

His men followed in silence, leaving Irene and Ang standing alone in the tense, suffocating quiet.

Ayden broke the silence with a mocking laugh. "Come on, everyone! Let's not let one drunken girl spoil the fun!"

The room slowly returned to its former noise and movement, though it lacked the previous intensity. The partygoers shifted awkwardly, resuming their conversations, while Ayden swaggered through the crowd, his heavy hips swaying as though nothing had happened.

06 CHASTITY

Embracing purity and self-control in one's sexual conduct, promoting respect for oneself and others, fostering deep emotional connections, and valuing intimacy within the context of commitment and love.

"Hey man! Sorry, I'm late," Azlan apologized to Abraham as he removed his backpack and placed it on an empty chair opposite him.

Abraham had been waiting at their favorite restaurant on the west coast beach, a place he loved for its view of the street and the sea. Since his breakup with Inara, this spot had become a refuge where he could sit with a drink and observe the world. He had eschewed alcohol to avoid becoming a cliché of heartbreak, but he felt uneasy occupying a table without ordering. He believed in spending proportionately to the time he spent in a restaurant. His family and friends had occasionally criticized him for what they perceived as excessive drinking, mistaking his coping mechanism for alcoholism. They expected him to be visibly upset, as if his pain was an opportunity for them to express their support.

But Abraham was a self-reliant individual who rarely sought help or advice from others. His perspective on life often puzzled those around him, leaving him with just one best friend: Azlan. Although Abraham had many friends,

Azlan was the only one who accepted him as he was without attempting to change him.

Abraham gave Azlan a mock frown, as Azlan was expected to arrive an hour earlier.

"Dude! Don't be an Indian with me. Try to be on time in the future."

Abraham got up from his chair and hugged Azlan, who responded with a tight embrace, ignoring the jest. They both settled into their seats, next to each other, facing the street and the sea.

"How are you?" Azlan asked, but his attention was quickly diverted to a woman walking across the street. She wore high pointy black heels, a dark gray suit with a short skirt, and her straightened hair flowed behind her like a cape. The weather hinted at an impending rainstorm.

Abraham also admired the woman, and he and Azlan exchanged a knowing look before they both chuckled.

"Yeah! Men will be men," Azlan laughed. "So, how are you?"

"Good. You?" Abraham responded. "Why the delay today?"

"You know, work. Not everyone is fortunate enough to have a job that allows them to hang out at a bar all day."

The waitress approached, handing Azlan a menu and smiling at Abraham.

"We'll have two beers, chicken 65, onion pakoda, and egg burji," Abraham said, taking the menu from Azlan and passing it back to the waitress.

The waitress adjusted her hair, took the menu, and left with a bright smile.

"Dude! She's totally into you," Azlan exclaimed as soon as she was out of earshot.

Abraham blushed but tried to downplay it. "Nothing like that, man. I've been coming here often; it's just a friendly smile."

"No way. The way she played with her hair and focused solely on you—that's flirting," Azlan insisted, nudging Abraham playfully.

"Come on, man! She's a waitress. I bet she's like that with all the customers. It's part of the job."

"Don't act like I don't know anything. She's definitely interested. You wouldn't lose anything by asking her out."

At that moment, the waitress returned with the beers and a plate of egg burji. She placed the beer in front of Azlan and the other beer and egg burji in front of Abraham, all the while giving Abraham another lingering smile before leaving.

Abraham completely ignored her and fixed his gaze on the beer.

"You're an asshole!" Azlan said, raising his glass in a toast.

Abraham looked at him, confused.

"She's clearly into you, and you're acting like a jerk. Is it too much to ask for you to be a little nice?" Azlan pressed.

"Dude! Calm down. Why are you so worked up?"

"I'm not angry, just frustrated. You're ignoring a pretty girl."

"Come on, man! She's just a kid," Abraham said, grimacing.

"She's definitely over twenty-one, probably in her mid-twenties."

"But you know my policy. I date girls within three years of my age."

"Yeah, that stupid policy. You don't know the global rule of half plus seven? You're thirty, so half is fifteen plus seven makes twenty-two. By that rule, you can date anyone twenty-two or older."

"Well, people have their own restrictions, and this is mine."

"What about Stella from work?"

"I have a policy against workplace romances. It's generally advised against."

"Okay, what about Susan from your improv theater?"

"Well…" Abraham hesitated, "you know my type. I'm not a fan of larger breasts. I'm not saying she's fat; just that her proportions are a bit much for me."

"What about Irene?" Azlan winked.

"Seriously? She's a good friend. I don't see her that way."

"Yeah, whatever!" Azlan leaned back in his chair, drink in hand, and stared out at the sea. "I think you should get laid."

"Dude!" Abraham reacted immediately. "I'm not going to have meaningless sex just because I'm single. For me, sex is something that should be filled with love and romance. I don't have sex; I make love."

The waitress returned with the remaining dishes, placing them on the table. This time, she left them on the empty side, giving Abraham one last, lingering smile before walking away.

"Thank you!" Abraham thanked her out loud with a smile as she walked away.

"See! Was that so hard?" Azlan asked.

They continued drinking their beers, gazing out at the sea.

"How are you?" Azlan asked calmly, still watching the waves.

"I'm okay," Abraham replied quietly. "Why do you ask again?"

"I don't know, man. Going through a breakup isn't easy. I was devastated in university, even over a short relationship. And you? After four years with Inara, you're acting like nothing happened. Don't you miss her?"

"Just because I'm not crying doesn't mean I'm not hurt," Abraham said, his voice breaking slightly.

They sat in silence, watching the sea.

"What happened between you two?" Azlan asked softly, turning to Abraham.

"I don't know, man." Abraham's voice broke further. He took a long sip of his drink, trying to steady his breathing. "We started drifting apart. When I moved here, we were on the phone all the time. We'd talk from when we woke up until one of us fell asleep. We'd find silly reasons to message each other, ask about meals, even discuss simple equations. We did it with 2G internet and waited patiently through frozen video calls. In the last year, even with 5G, she complained about traffic noise. Weeks passed without calls, months without meeting. I anticipated the breakup for a while. Maybe that's why it wasn't as hard as it could have been. Sometimes, I wish I were more like others so I could experience the pain more intensely and cry."

Abraham wiped away a tear, trying to hide it from Azlan. Although Azlan noticed, he chose to remain silent and let Abraham process his feelings.

"You still love her?" Azlan asked, breaking the silence.

Abraham remained silent, fearing his voice would collapse into tears. He didn't want to cry in his favorite restaurant.

"I still care for her. I care for almost everyone I know, but I care for her more. If that's love, then yes, I still love her. I want what's best for her. If that's love, then yes, I still love her. I still feel pain when she does, and I want her to be happy. If you call all this love, then yes, I still love her," Abraham said, his voice rising with emotion. "But I also feel the same way about you."

Azlan stayed silent, respecting Abraham's need to express his emotions. He knew better than to push too hard.

"But do you miss her? Not just in a general sense, but specifically?" Azlan asked, knowing Abraham's tendency to deflect.

A tear escaped Abraham's eye. Azlan, without a word, gently rubbed Abraham's back. They sat in silence for several minutes.

"So, what really happened between you two?" Azlan asked. "We never talked about it. It seemed like everything was fine, and then suddenly, you were separated."

"Thinking about it, I guess I was the asshole. She said…"

"No, I don't want to hear her side. I want to know what you think went wrong," Azlan interrupted, encouraging Abraham to own his part of the story.

"Well, she said I was judgmental, and I agree with that. I was going through a tough time, didn't share my feelings, and felt my knowledge wasn't appreciated. I might have been jealous of her success in quantum physics, despite my own achievements. I think I made a comment about Alejandro that might have been aimed at her. I was jealous of her success and might have pushed her to slow down, though I was genuinely concerned for her mental health. I shouldn't have tried to help her when I wasn't clear about myself."

Abraham stopped to take a deep breath and lit a cigarette.

"So, active listening, empathy—those issues I have at work were the same reasons I was a jerk to her. She shared her motivations late, and I don't remember them well because I was depressed myself."

Azlan listened quietly, allowing Abraham to express himself fully. Though he couldn't get the full picture of what happened, he could understand the feelings behind Abraham's story and could see that Abraham was feeling sorry for his actions.

"I think she asked if I'd be with her through everything, or something like that. I don't remember clearly," Abraham said, scratching his head.

"Focus. Forget what she wanted from you. You were a jerk, but you've changed. Those improv lessons seem to have helped," Azlan said.

Abraham nodded, stashing his cigarette in the ashtray.

"So, let me ask you again. Do you still love her?" Azlan asked.

Abraham nodded again.

"If you had another chance with her—if she still loved you and wanted to be with you—would you go back to her?"

"In a heartbeat," Abraham replied without hesitation. But his voice softened as he continued, "But she's dating Alejandro now. There's nothing I can do except accept it and move on. I need a bit more time, but I'll be fine."

"That jerk? Why?" Azlan exclaimed, but they both knew it was rhetorical. They continued drinking in silence.

"Well, he is charismatic, and openly appreciates her intelligence. Supports her drive. He has been a very good business partner. I guess he will be a good life partner to her as well," Abraham shared his thoughts, a faint smile playing on his lips as if he had come to terms with the reality.

Azlan nodded slowly, but the tension between them hung in the air for a moment. Abraham broke the silence, as if he had said all that needed to be said.

"Anyway, how's Irem and my goddaughter, Ieasha?"

"Iea's good. She's getting naughtier. She used to ask about

you a lot, but you haven't visited in a while, and she's starting to forget you. You should come by sometime."

"Sure. I'll be there for her birthday next weekend, I promise. How's Irem?"

"Ah, she's fine too," Azlan replied disinterestedly.

"Do you guys still fight?"

Azlan took a long sip of his drink and lit a cigarette. Abraham did the same.

"I don't know what she wants from me, man. I left my family for her. I hardly visit or even talk to my parents. They're old, and I'm their only son. I should be taking care of them. Instead, I abandoned them for Irem."

Abraham nodded, sensing the weight of Azlan's guilt. "That's rough, man. It must have been the toughest choice to make."

"Yeah, I know. But still, it eats at me. Yes, my mom shouldn't have acted like a tele-novela mother-in-law, but I feel guilty for leaving them. Marriage isn't just about creating a third family, it's about merging two families. Why can't people understand that? I think we forgot to pass on this important aspect of our culture somewhere when we were too busy fighting for our freedom."

Azlan finished his cigarette and took another deep sip of his drink. Abraham listened, appreciating Azlan's insight despite the pain it caused him.

"Don't get married, man. Seriously. It'll take away all your peace."

Abraham smiled faintly but waited for him to continue.

"If it weren't for Iea, I'd have left everything or gone insane by now," Azlan said, his voice quieter. "Having her was a mistake at first, but now… she's the only thing keeping me grounded."

"I can't imagine how tough that is," Abraham said, trying to empathize before lightening the mood. "But you know, the grass is always greener on the other side." He chuckled softly, trying to ease the tension.

"Yeah, it reminds me of a message I saw: Marriage is like a public toilet. People outside desperately want to get in, while those inside just want to get out."

They both laughed.

"Okay, man. After this, I'm heading out," Azlan said, signaling the end of the evening.

"So early? It's only nine."

"Yeah, I know," Azlan sighed, clearly not thrilled about it. "Irem wants to go shopping tomorrow, and if I don't go, I'll never hear the end of it. Why can't we just do it on Sunday? But you know how it is," he added, rolling his eyes slightly.

07 SLOTH

A habitual disinclination to exertion, resulting in laziness, idleness, and a failure to fulfill one's duties and responsibilities, both to oneself and to society, leading to stagnation and wasted potential.

"Hey man! Sorry, I'm late." Azlan apologized to Abraham as he removed his backpack and placed it on an empty chair opposite Abraham.

Abraham had been waiting at their favorite restaurant on the west coast beach, a place he loved for its view of the street and the sea. Since his breakup with Inara, this spot had become a refuge where he could sit with a drink and observe the world. He had eschewed alcohol to avoid becoming a cliché of heartbreak, but he felt uneasy occupying a table without ordering. He believed in spending proportionately to the time he spent in a restaurant. His family and friends had occasionally criticized him for what they perceived as excessive drinking, mistaking his coping mechanism for alcoholism. They expected him to be visibly upset, as if his pain was an opportunity for them to express their support.

But Abraham was a self-reliant individual who rarely sought help or advice from others. His perspective on life often puzzled those around him, leaving him with just one best friend: Azlan. Although Abraham had many friends,

Azlan was the only one who accepted him as he was without attempting to change him.

Abraham gave Azlan a mock frown, as Azlan was expected to arrive an hour earlier.

"Dude! Don't be an Indian with me. Try to be on time in future."

Abraham got up from his chair and hugged Azlan, who responded with a tight embrace, ignoring the jest. They both settled into their seats, next to each other and facing the street and the sea.

"How are you?" Azlan asked Abraham, but his attention was quickly diverted to a woman walking across the street. She wore high pointy black heels, a dark gray suit with a short skirt, and her straightened hair flowed behind her like a cape. The weather hinted at an impending rainstorm.

Abraham also admired the woman, and he and Azlan exchanged a knowing look before they both chuckled.

"Yeah! Men will be men," Azlan laughed. "So, how are you?"

"Good. You?" Abraham responded. "Why the delay today?"

"You know, work. Not everyone is fortunate enough to have a job that allows them to hang out at a bar all day."

The waitress approached, handing Azlan a menu and smiling at Abraham.

"We'll have two beers, chicken 65, onion pakoda, and egg burji," Abraham said, taking the menu from Azlan and passing it back to the waitress.

The waitress adjusted her hair, took the menu, and left with a bright smile.

"Dude! She's totally into you," Azlan exclaimed as soon as she was out of earshot.

"Dude! Calm down. Why are you so worked up?" Abraham tried to soothe Azlan, then added with a sly grin, "Even I was into her last night, if you know what I mean." Abraham winked mischievously at Azlan.

"Whaaaat...?" Azlan exclaimed quietly, eyes wide with disbelief. "You dog! Isn't she like twenty or something? Isn't that a bit young for you?"

"You mean the three-year difference? Forget about it. She's over eighteen, I think." He paused, his gaze drifting as he briefly considered the consequences if she wasn't as old as he thought. A hint of uncertainty crossed his face, but after a moment, he shrugged it off with a slight smirk. "But honestly, who cares anymore?"

At that moment, the waitress returned with the beers and a plate of egg burji. She placed the beer in front of Azlan and the other beer and egg burji in front of Abraham, all the while giving Abraham another lingering smile before leaving.

Abraham completely ignored her and fixed his gaze on the beer.

Azlan glanced around to make sure no one could overhear them before continuing. As he turned back, he winced and clutched the back of his neck, groaning in discomfort.

"That sounds like a cervicogenic headache," Abraham said, sounding somewhat knowledgeable. "Usually from poor posture or muscle strain. Just use your beer as a cold compress."

"I don't think it's that. Cervicogenic headaches are typically one-sided and might extend to the forehead in severe cases. This pain is more diffuse across my entire head, though it's pretty mild," Azlan explained, moving the beer glass around his neck and head to soothe the discomfort.

"You're right," Abraham admitted after a moment's thought. "I had something similar when I was with Susan."

"What do you mean?" Azlan asked, leaning in with curiosity.

"You remember Susan?" Abraham said with a sheepish smile.

"Yeah, from the improv group. The one with—" Azlan gestured to indicate her unusually large breasts.

"Yeah, her. We ended up alone for drinks, and let's just say we explored a bit more than just the bar menu," Abraham said, his grin widening.

"You dog!" Azlan said, laughing and adding a playful

howl. "But isn't she completely opposite of your usual type?"

"Yes, but I don't care about those criteria anymore," Abraham replied, taking a sip of his beer. "Even with Stella…"

"Don't tell me you hooked up with her too," Azlan interrupted, incredulous.

"Right there in the office," Abraham said nonchalantly, taking another swig of his beer.

The waitress returned with the remaining dishes, placing them on the table. This time, she left them on the empty side, giving Abraham another smile before walking away. Abraham winked back at her.

Azlan remained silent, trying to mask his disbelief. The Abraham sitting across from him wasn't the friend he knew—this carefree playboy attitude felt unfamiliar, and Azlan struggled with how to respond. He continued drinking his beer, gazing out at the sea.

"How are you?" Azlan asked calmly, still watching the waves.

"I'm okay," Abraham replied quietly. "Why do you ask again?"

"I don't know, man. Going through a breakup isn't easy. I was devastated in university, even over a short relationship. And you? After four years with Inara, you're acting like nothing happened. Don't you miss her?"

"Just because I'm not crying doesn't mean I'm not hurt," Abraham said, his voice breaking slightly.

They sat in silence, watching the sea.

"What happened between you two?" Azlan asked softly, turning to Abraham.

"I don't know, man," Abraham muttered, his voice both strained and subdued. He took a long sip of his drink, trying to steady his breathing. "We started drifting apart. I think making money and looking pretty and slim seemed more important to her than a long-distance relationship with an Indian guy. Maybe she needed more than just words and promises in a relationship," Abraham's voice darkened. "Maybe that's why she jumped right into that jerk's arms."

"Who?" Azlan enquired.

Abraham looked inside the restaurant, and the waitress immediately noticed him. It was like she was always keeping an eye on Abraham. Abraham signaled by raising two fingers that he needed two more beers, completely ignoring the shine in her eyes.

"Alejandro," Abraham replied to Azlan, taking his own sweet time, as he lit a cigarette.

"That jerk? Why?" Azlan exclaimed, lighting a cigarette for himself as well.

"Why do you think?" Abraham continued. "He's rich, not Indian, white-skinned. What more do you think an Indian girl needs? That bitch just couldn't wait to move on," Abraham fumed, lighting another cigarette.

Azlan felt uncomfortable. Firstly, because of how his best friend was behaving like a total jerk and, second, his headache kept growing.

Azlan decided to continue his drink and cigarette in silence. Abraham remained silent as well, fearing the rage he was controlling might come out as tears, and Azlan might interpret it as him missing Inara.

Azlan wasn't stupid when it came to emotions. He knew that Abraham missed Inara and that, somewhere, he got confused with his emotions and made a choice to be angry at her. And in that anger, he was lashing out by using words he would never normally use in his life.

Azlan watched him for a moment before speaking softly. "You're still hung up on her, aren't you?"

Abraham remained silent, fearing his voice would collapse into tears. He didn't want to cry in his favorite restaurant.

"I still care for her. I care for almost everyone I know, but I care for her more. If that's love, then yes, I still love her. I want what's best for her. If that's love, then yes, I still love her. I still feel pain when she does, and I want her to be happy. If you call all this love, then yes, I still love her," Abraham said, his voice rising with emotion. "But I also feel the same way about you."

Azlan stayed silent, respecting Abraham's need to express

his emotions. He knew better than to push too hard. He also stayed silent because a dull throb had pulsed through his head again. He rubbed the back of his neck, hoping the growing discomfort wasn't showing on his face.

"But do you miss her? Not just in a general sense, but specifically?" Azlan asked, knowing Abraham's tendency to deflect.

A tear escaped Abraham's eye. Azlan, without a word, gently rubbed Abraham's back. They sat in silence for several minutes.

"So, what really happened between you two?" Azlan asked. "We never talked about it. It seemed like everything was fine, and then suddenly, you were separated."

"Thinking about it, people call me…"

"I don't want to know what people think of you. I know you. I want to know what you think went wrong," Azlan interrupted, encouraging Abraham to own his part of the story.

"Well, people called me an asshole. And I have to agree with them now for two reasons. First, I was going through a tough time, didn't share my feelings, and felt my knowledge wasn't appreciated. I might have been jealous of her success in quantum physics, despite my own achievements. I think I made a comment about Alejandro that might have been aimed at her. I was jealous of her success and might have pushed her to slow down, though I was genuinely concerned for her mental health. I shouldn't have tried to help her when I wasn't clear about myself."

Abraham stopped to take a deep breath and lit a cigarette.

"So, active listening, empathy—those issues I have at work were the same reasons I was a jerk to her. She shared her motivations late, and I don't remember them well because I was depressed myself."

Azlan listened quietly, allowing Abraham to express himself fully. Though he couldn't get the full picture of what happened, he could understand the feelings behind Abraham's story and see that Abraham was sorry for his actions.

"That leads to my second reason. On the day I broke up with her, I found a piece of paper in which I wrote 'Listen to her during the call and never interrupt her.' To be honest, I don't remember writing that. Maybe I wrote it when I was drunk during the week when we were on a break before the breakup. I don't know. But what is important is, I interrupted her. I didn't let her finish her thought. The last words from her were 'people don't change,' and I proved her right. Once an A-hole, and I will always be one, I guess," Abraham concluded, stashing his unsmoked cigarette in the ashtray.

Azlan, having no words, remained silent. They continued to drink in silence.

"Anyway, how's Irem and my goddaughter, Ieasha?"

"Iea's good. She's getting naughtier. She used to ask about you a lot, but you haven't visited in a while, and she's starting to forget you. You should come by sometime."

"Sure. I'll be there for her birthday next weekend, I promise. How's Irem?"

"Ah, she's fine too," Azlan replied disinterestedly.

"Do you guys still fight?"

Azlan took a long sip of his drink and lit a cigarette. Abraham did the same.

"I don't know what she wants from me, man. I left my family for her. I hardly visit or even talk to my parents. They're old, and I'm their only son. I should be taking care of them. Instead, I abandoned them for Irem."

Abraham nodded, sensing the weight of Azlan's guilt. "That's rough, man. It must have been the toughest choice to make."

"Yeah, I know. But still, it eats at me. Yes, my mom shouldn't have acted like a tele-novela mother-in-law, but I feel guilty for leaving them. Marriage isn't just about creating a third family, it's about merging two families. Why can't people understand that? I think we forgot to pass on this important aspect of our culture somewhere when we were too busy fighting for our freedom."

Azlan finished his cigarette and took another deep sip of his drink, but a sudden sharp pulse of pain cut through his head, making him wince slightly. He rubbed his temples, hoping Abraham wouldn't notice, and forced a smile. The headache had grown more insistent, but he pushed it aside.

Abraham listened, appreciating Azlan's insight despite the pain it caused him.

"Don't get married, man. Seriously. It'll take away all your peace."

Abraham smiled faintly but waited for him to continue.

"If it weren't for Iea, I'd have left everything or gone insane by now," Azlan said, his voice quieter. "Having her was a mistake at first, but now… she's the only thing keeping me grounded."

"I can't imagine how tough that is," Abraham said, trying to empathize before lightening the mood. "But you know, the grass is always greener on the other side." He chuckled softly, trying to ease the tension.

"Yeah, it reminds me of a message I saw: Marriage is like a public toilet. People outside desperately want to get in, while those inside just want to get out."

They both laughed.

"Okay, man. After this, I'm heading out," Azlan said, signaling the end of the evening.

"So early? It's only nine."

"Yeah, I know," Azlan sighed, clearly not thrilled about it. "Irem wants to go shopping tomorrow, and if I don't go, I'll never hear the end of it. Why can't we just do it on Sunday? But you know how it is," he added, rolling his eyes slightly.

08 GREED

An intense and selfish desire for wealth, power, or possessions, often resulting in unethical behavior, exploitation, and a disregard for the well-being of others and moral principles.

"What are you going to do about it, Chief?"

A man standing among the crowd in the shack raised his voice, loud enough for Ang and everyone else to hear. His question pierced the room, followed by a sudden, heavy silence.

The prayer hall, emptied of its usual furniture, was packed with villagers. The air was thick with tension, the incense stick still faintly burning from the morning prayer. Despite the extra space, not everyone could fit inside, with many standing outside, trying to catch snippets of the conversation.

The Buddha statue at the end of the hall seemed to loom larger than usual, watching over the gathering in stillness. Ang stood in front of it, a calm pillar amidst the rising anxiety.

"Chief, you don't need to explain what happened. We know Irene wouldn't have acted without good reason," a man from the front spoke, offering support to Ang.

"But it's her actions that have put us in this situation," the man from the crowd countered, his persistence creating tension in the air.

"This would've happened eventually, regardless of what Irene did," the man in the front argued. "Maybe not today, maybe not in the same way, but Ayden has been looking for an excuse to bring us down. We're his biggest threat." His voice rang with conviction, and murmurs of agreement echoed through the crowd.

Some heads turned, nodding; others shifted uncomfortably as the weight of the situation sank in.

"But she was the one at the party, representing the village! She should've been more careful, more aware of the consequences. Just because she's the Chief's daughter doesn't mean she automatically gets the right to attend," the persistent man continued, his voice gaining momentum. The crowd responded, some murmuring in agreement.

Ang's gaze moved slowly across the room, sensing the wavering loyalties, the frustration brewing. He stood calmly, silently observing the debate and the crowd's shifting sentiments. He could sense them leaning toward blaming Irene. Still, he remained quiet, knowing that defending his daughter too quickly might be seen as biased. He let the incense swirl in front of him, waiting for the right moment to speak.

"She didn't go to represent the village," the man at the front clarified. "She went because the Governor invited the chiefs and their families. She went because, as the Chief's daughter, it would've been seen as an insult to refuse. She agreed to attend, even though she didn't want to, because we convinced her it was the right thing to do at the time."

The crowd fell silent, and the man in the crowd pushing the blame seemed to realize he wasn't helping. He, too, went quiet.

Ang seized the moment. "Do not dwell in the past, do not dream of the future, concentrate the mind on the present moment," he quoted. "Buddha taught us that. It doesn't mean we ignore the past or fail to plan for the future, but we must focus on what we do next."

Nods of agreement rippled through the crowd as the

tension eased.

The low hum of agreement from the villagers gave Ang the momentum he needed.

"His demand is unreasonable, yes. But does he have the right to make such a demand? Unfortunately, he does," Ang continued, his voice soft but firm. "What are his demands? Fifty bags of rice by Wednesday for the insult at his party. Is that fair? The law says he can ask for it. And if we don't comply, the one who caused the insult has to serve him for a year. We all know what that means for Irene, and why the Governor wants it. But are we going to let that happen?"

He paused, letting his words sink in as he scanned the room. No one objected, but confusion lingered on their faces. They didn't know how to solve the problem. The soft crackle of the incense was the only sound in the hall now.

"But Chief, how can we deliver fifty bags of rice by Wednesday?" a man from the crowd spoke up. "We only have forty, and that's barely enough to get us through the winter. The other villages won't help us—they don't want to cross the Governor. And we don't have time to bring rice from far away. Even if we tried, the Governor would stop it at the borders, claiming customs issues."

A woman near the door whispered to her neighbor, "How can we survive the winter without our rice?"

All eyes turned to Ang.

"But we can't let Irene be enslaved!" the man in the front urged. "Without her, the Governor will push us back to where we were before she brought progress to the village. Remember, your son is in school because of her work. Do you want him back on the farm?"

More murmurs followed—this time louder, filled with fear and uncertainty.

Ang remained quiet, letting the reality of the situation sink in. "I'm at an impasse," he finally said. "As Chief, I cannot ask you to give up the rice that we have, knowing it's all we have for winter. But at the same time, I cannot send my daughter to serve the Governor. I see no other option but to step down and let someone else make this decision."

His words sent a wave of shock through the room. The crowd erupted into anxious whispers.

"No one in their right mind could make that choice!" someone shouted.

"Sacrifice one to save the village," another voice called out. Some glared at the speaker, while others, reluctantly, nodded.

The weight of that sacrifice settled over the room, suffocating the small hope some still held.

Irene, who had been standing silently among the crowd, finally stepped forward. Moving beside Ang, she raised her voice, commanding attention. "No one saves us but ourselves. No one can and no one may. We ourselves must walk the path."

Her voice silenced the crowd, and all eyes turned to her.

She repeated, more softly this time, "No one saves us but ourselves. No one can and no one may. We ourselves must walk the path. Buddha said that. No matter how much we defend it, I am responsible for putting us in this situation."

Ang stared at her, his mind racing, unsure of what she was doing. The crowd watched her, their hope and confusion palpable.

"I don't want anyone else to make this difficult decision," she continued, her voice steady. "There's no need for you to step down." She turned to her father, meeting his eyes with calm assurance. "I will find a way to fix this without us losing a single bag of rice. If I can't, I'll go to the Governor on my own."

Her words were a heavy declaration, but Irene's face was set in stone—resolute, unyielding.

The crowd began to murmur again, processing the weight of her words.

Ang leaned in, speaking softly to her. "You don't have to do this. I'd rather step down than watch him destroy you."

Irene took her father's hands, holding them gently. "No, Papa. I'm not doing this for you. I've dedicated my life to saving this village, and I won't stand by and let Ayden destroy it. But trust me, I won't let it come to that."

INNOCENCE

The wind swept across the dry, cracked seabed, stirring up small dust clouds where waves had once lapped the shore. Adrien and Andre sat on the balcony of a small, weathered beach house, their chairs positioned to face the remnants of the ocean. The chairs creaked slightly with each shift in weight, and the rustling wind filled the silence between them.

There was no water left—not a trace of the once vibrant blue expanse that had defined the west coast of France. Now, the ocean floor stretched out like a barren desert, an endless landscape of parched earth, fractured by the heat. Sunlight refracted off the scorched surface, casting a shimmering, mirage-like haze that made the horizon flicker and fade in the distance.

"It's strange, isn't it? How the ocean just... vanished," Adrien said, his eyes scanning the barren seabed. "I don't understand the physics behind it. Isn't the water level controlled by the Moon?"

Andre glanced at him, slightly amused but appreciating Adrien's curiosity. "That's a common misconception," he began, his voice calm and measured. "The Moon's gravitational pull does affect the water, yes, but it's not as simple as the phases of the Moon controlling the waves."

Adrien tilted his head, listening intently.

"Here's the thing," Andre continued, turning to face the dry expanse before them. "The Moon's gravity pulls on Earth's oceans, causing the water to bulge out on the side closest to the Moon. That's why we get high tides. But what people don't realize is that there's another bulge on the opposite side of the planet—away from the Moon."

"What?" Adrien blinked, surprised. "Why would there be a bulge on the other side too?"

"Balance," Andre said with a nod. "While the Moon pulls water toward itself, the Earth and Moon are actually rotating around a common center of mass. The centrifugal force from that motion causes water to bulge on the far side as well. So, in effect, you have two high tides at the same time—one on the side facing the Moon, and one on the opposite side."

"That's… kind of crazy," Adrien admitted. "But it makes sense."

Andre's expression darkened as he continued. "The oceans are constantly shifting to maintain balance on Earth. They move with the Earth's rotation, always adjusting to the pull of the Moon. It's nature's way of keeping the planet stable—preventing it from wobbling or becoming unstable."

Adrien's fingers absently traced the rim of his glass as he thought it over. "And now… with the ocean gone, that balance is broken."

Andre's gaze swept across the scorched seabed. "Well, the ocean isn't really gone. We tipped the scales. The water's been pulled away from here to try and keep the Earth balanced. It's gathered on the other side of the planet, but that's caused its own set of problems."

"We screwed it up," Adrien blurted out, but immediately regretted his words. He had been trying to keep Andre from darker thoughts, but now, he had let his own slip.

A heavy silence followed. The wind whispered faintly, swirling dust from the dry seabed and carrying it into the air like ghosts of waves long vanished. Andre let out a slow breath, leaning forward in his chair, elbows resting on his knees.

"It was a challenging decision. And we followed the protocol," Andre said softly, trying to absolve them both of the guilt that weighed so heavily.

Adrien looked at him. Their eyes met in a silent exchange, each acknowledging the other's attempt to lift the burden of self-blame, though both still carried it within.

"Try telling that to South America." Adrien sighed, his voice weary. "Oh wait, we can't. They're underwater."

His tone wasn't sarcastic, but reflective of the back-and-forth dialogue they often used to challenge each other. They had developed a method where one always took the opposing side, no matter the situation, to critically weigh the pros and cons of their decisions. It had served them well in the past, helping them make clear-headed choices. Now, however, the weight of their actions felt unbearable, even if it had once seemed like the right call.

"We didn't foresee this," Andre said quietly. "The greatest threat we saw was India and China breaking from the international treaty if we didn't inform them. Protocol was the only path forward."

"Yeah," Adrien agreed, the bitterness fading from his voice. "There's no way we could have known it would lead to... this." He gestured toward the barren seabed. "And even they didn't see it coming. Now we can't even question them. They're submerged under their own damn decisions."

Andre leaned back in his chair, closing his eyes against the harsh sunlight. "Let's just enjoy what's left," he said, his voice steady but hollow. "Blaming anyone won't help anymore."

Adrien's grip tightened around his glass as the wind howled faintly, filling the space between them. Andre opened his eyes and turned toward Adrien. "It's too late even to analyze it."

Adrien stared at him, searching for some reassurance, but found none. The ocean was gone, and the world they had known seemed to be slipping further away with each passing moment.

He picked up his glass and drained the last of the wine in one slow gulp. "Too late," he echoed softly.

The sun dipped lower in the sky, casting long shadows over the parched earth. The waves that had once roared and crashed along the shore were now nothing more than distant memories, lost in the dust and heat of an empty world.

09 WRATH

Intense anger and hatred that manifest in destructive actions, words, and thoughts, harming others and oneself, and often leading to violence, revenge, and a breakdown of relationships and community harmony.

"Where the hell are you?" Irem muttered under her breath, glancing at her daughter standing beside her.

The mall was unusually crowded that Saturday. The dark clouds and persistent drizzle had cast a gloomy atmosphere over the city, only adding to Irem's frustration as she waited outside the mall for her husband to pick them up.

The seven-story mall, a popular destination for the middle and upper-middle classes, offered affordable luxury with its wide range of shops, an open food court, and a kids' play zone. Unfortunately, the rainy weather had driven more people indoors than usual, making the air conditioning nearly ineffective. The result was a chaotic, sweaty crowd, with cranky children and equally irritable adults.

With everyone opting to drive due to the rain, the streets were jammed with cars. Those without cars faced high demand for taxis and auto-rickshaws, leading to heated negotiations between drivers and passengers. The traffic congestion only worsened the situation outside the mall.

Turning slightly away from her daughter, Irem continued

in a hushed but irate tone, "I've been standing here with all these bags for ten minutes. Ieasha is getting drenched!"

She listened to the response from the other end, her eyes scanning the chaotic traffic in front of her. Her frustration boiled over.

"Don't tell me to calm down! If you'd waited just five more minutes for me to finish paying, we wouldn't be in this mess. You spend hours partying with your friends, but you can't spare five minutes for your wife and daughter? If you care so little, why did you even marry me? Why make our daughter suffer too?"

Azlan took a deep breath as he spotted the mall's entrance through the sea of traffic. The congestion eased slightly, allowing him to move a few meters forward. He allowed himself to relax for just a moment, basking in the fleeting harmony that hung in the air. But just as he settled back, the ground seemed to shift beneath him—a reminder that he was late. Through the windows, he saw Irem struggling with an armful of shopping bags and holding their daughter, Ieasha, by the hand. Ieasha was happily munching on an ice cream cone, seemingly oblivious to her mother's irritation. Irem's struggle to manage the bags while keeping Ieasha close and handling the phone was evident.

Azlan felt a twinge of guilt for snapping at her earlier. She wasn't perfect, but she was always doing her best. And in that moment, watching her care for their daughter amid the crowd, he realized how much she held everything together. He realized that, while she might not be the ideal wife, she was undoubtedly the best mother he could hope for.

"Okay, I can see you. Can you see me?" Azlan asked, pausing for her response. "Try to come down to the car. Don't worry about the traffic; everyone is crazy here." He smiled, hoping she could sense his reassurance even if she couldn't see it.

Irem put her phone away, shifted the bags to her other hand, and began descending the stairs toward the road.

Azlan's focus on his wife was momentarily interrupted by a car behind him honking impatiently, signaling him to move.

He tossed his phone onto the dashboard and drove forward.

"Bloody hell! Not even letting me admire my own wife," he grumbled to himself.

He pulled up directly in front of the mall, amidst the traffic, and leaned down to see Irem and Ieasha approaching.

Ieasha spotted her father and waved her ice cream cone at him, but the gesture caused the ice cream to fall off. She stopped, looking up at her mother. Irem's anger towards Azlan softened when she saw Ieasha's disappointed face, and she managed a smile.

"I'll get you a new one when we get home, okay? Let's go now," Irem said, smiling at Azlan.

Azlan felt a surge of relief and a fleeting sense of optimism. He thought to himself, "Looks like I'm getting some tonight," reassured by Irem's smile.

Suddenly, a deafening explosion shattered the relative calm. The air around him seemed to split open with a deafening roar. The ground shook as if the earth itself had cracked. The glass wall of the mall's first floor exploded outward in a shower of shards. Panicked screams erupted from inside the building as people began to flee. Irem dropped the shopping bags, grabbed Ieasha tightly and started running toward the car.

Azlan scrambled to open the car door, desperate for Irem and Ieasha to get inside and escape the chaos. Just as he reached for the seat belt buckle, a second, far more powerful explosion rocked the building.

The force of the blast sent a metal stand careening through the air, its frame twisting violently. Laden with clothes, the stand hurtled toward Irem. She ducked instinctively, narrowly avoiding the deadly debris. Azlan felt the ground shift beneath him again, but this time in a terrifying way—panic tightening in his chest.

As the metal stand flew past Irem, it continued its trajectory directly toward Azlan's car. At first, he saw only the clothes flapping wildly in the wind. But then, his heart lurched as he made out a horrifying detail among the debris: his daughter, Ieasha, was caught in the metal frame.

One moment, Ieasha was at Irem's side, her tiny hand gripping her mother's, and the next, a blast of air hurled her backward. The metal frame caught her like a snare, dragging her helpless body into its twisted embrace as it soared toward Azlan's car. The full horror of the situation dawned on him—Ieasha was being thrust toward the car, trapped in the metal stand with the clothes swirling around her. The scene was surreal and nightmarish. Azlan's heart pounded as he realized that Ieasha was on a collision course with the shattered window of his car.

He watched, paralyzed with fear and anguish, as Ieasha's small form was flung through the air. He wanted to scream, to move, to do something—anything—but his body betrayed him. His heart pounded in his chest, each beat more excruciating than the last, as if time had slowed just to stretch out the agony of the moment. The sight of his daughter, helpless and vulnerable, being hurled toward him through the chaos was agonizing. The realization that she would not survive the impact overwhelmed him.

Azlan's eyes remained fixed on the approaching disaster, even as shards of glass and fragments of the metal frame flew toward him. His gaze was locked on Ieasha, and he could do nothing but witness the horror unfolding before him. The scene was a heart-wrenching tableau of destruction, with Ieasha's fate hanging in the balance.

He couldn't look away as glass, blood, and flesh hurtled toward him. His daughter's fate was sealed, and there was nothing he could do. He kept watching without blinking, even as the shattered window glass, along with the blood and fragments of flesh, flew toward him. The full horror of his daughter's impending fate was seared into his mind, rendering him utterly helpless in the face of the devastating reality.

10 PATIENCE

Cultivating the ability to endure difficult circumstances with a calm and composed demeanor, showing tolerance and understanding towards others, and maintaining hope and perseverance through adversity and hardship.

Azlan slowly drifted back to consciousness, his body feeling heavy, like a weight was pressing him into the bed. He tried to move, but it wasn't just physical—there was a mental fog, an overwhelming restraint, as if his mind and body were disconnected. His limbs wouldn't obey him. His eyelids fluttered, and his vision gradually sharpened, revealing the sterile white walls and machines of a hospital room. The air smelled faintly of antiseptic, and the rhythmic beeping of monitors was the only sound.

Abraham was there, seated in a chair beside his bed, elbows propped on his knees, supporting his head with his hands. His eyes were closed, but they snapped open at the sound of a faint moan escaping Azlan's lips. He sat up instantly, his eyes filling with concern.

Azlan's breathing quickened as his body stirred, but he still felt that strange, suffocating restraint, like a weight in his chest. Panic shot through him, and the machines monitoring his vitals responded with louder beeps, reflecting his distress.

Abraham was by his side in an instant, placing a hand

gently on his shoulder, guiding him back down onto the bed. "Easy, easy," he said softly, his voice steady but laced with concern. "Don't try to move too much yet. Just breathe. Take it slow, okay?"

But Azlan's mind was racing now, his heart pounding. He tried to speak, his voice rough and barely a whisper, but the urgency was unmistakable. "Ieasha?" The word slipped out, trembling with fear, his body tensing against the restraint.

Abraham's face tightened with sadness, his grip on Azlan's hand firm but gentle. He looked away briefly, as if gathering himself, before meeting Azlan's eyes again.

Before he could answer, a nurse hurried into the room, alerted by the machines. She quickly assessed the situation, her expression calm and practiced. "You were in an accident," she said softly, approaching Azlan with a reassuring smile. "There were shards of glass, but we've removed them, and you're stable now. Just try to relax. The doctor will be with you shortly."

Azlan's chest tightened further, the weight of her words doing little to ease his anxiety. He glanced at Abraham again, desperation now etched into his features. "Ieasha... Irem?" His voice was quieter this time, almost as if he feared the answer.

Abraham took a deep breath, his own eyes misting over, and he shook his head. "I'm sorry, man," he said, his voice breaking. "They didn't make it."

Azlan's whole body went still. The mental restraint he'd felt since waking now turned into something far worse—an unbearable emptiness. Tears welled up in his eyes, streaming silently down his cheeks. His breathing became shallow, his chest rising and falling rapidly, but there was no way to express the storm of pain inside him. The grief swallowed him whole.

Abraham squeezed Azlan's hand, trying to offer some small comfort, even though he knew nothing could truly help. The silence between them was thick, suffocating, as the reality settled in.

The nurse, sensing the intensity of the moment, gave a

final glance at the machines and quietly left the room, leaving the two men alone.

"I should have waited," Azlan whispered after a long pause, his voice trembling with guilt. "I shouldn't have left them. If they'd been with me... they'd be safe now." The tears continued, uncontrollable, his body wracked with silent sobs.

"It's not your fault," Abraham said softly, though he knew his words would never ease the pain. "You couldn't have known, Azlan. No one could have known."

Azlan's grip on Abraham's hand tightened. "For a quick smoke," he choked out, his voice breaking. "I left them for a smoke."

Abraham could only watch helplessly as his best friend fell apart in front of him, consumed by grief and guilt. He wanted to say something—anything—that could make it better. But he knew there were no words for this.

The phone in Abraham's pocket buzzed, vibrating loudly in the tense silence. He glanced down at the screen, hesitated for a moment, then declined the call. The timing was wrong. His place was here, with Azlan.

Azlan lay back on the bed, his tears still flowing, though he no longer had the strength to speak. His mind was racing, replaying every moment of the explosion. He could still see Irem and Ieasha, running toward him, and then... the blast. The metal frame. Ieasha's small body being tossed into the air. The terror in her eyes.

Abraham sat back down in his chair, his head in his hands, trying to hold it together. He didn't want to leave Azlan's side, but he could feel the weight of everything pressing down on him too.

"What happened?" Azlan asked, his voice a strained whisper.

Abraham raised his head, and for a moment, he hesitated. Then, with a deep breath, he spoke. "Terrorist attack," he said quietly, his voice thick with grief. "Two bombs. One inside the mall, another at the entrance." He paused, his heart sinking as he remembered the chaos of that day. "They didn't have a chance, Azlan. No one did."

Azlan closed his eyes, the memory of that moment now burned into his mind. His daughter's laughter, the feel of her hand in his. Gone in an instant. The overwhelming sense of guilt returned, suffocating him.

"You should rest," Abraham said gently, seeing the exhaustion etched across Azlan's face.

Azlan didn't respond. He lay there, staring at the ceiling, the weight of everything crushing him. There was no escape from this. No waking up from this nightmare.

"Where are they now?" Azlan asked, his voice weak but clear.

Abraham hesitated, a confused frown forming. He gripped Azlan's hand a little tighter, unsure how to respond. "They're... they didn't make it, Azlan," Abraham repeated softly, as if Azlan hadn't fully understood before.

"I know," Azlan said, his voice barely a whisper, his eyes closed. "I mean... their bodies. Where are their bodies?"

Abraham exhaled, understanding dawning. "They're still with the police," he replied quietly, his voice steady but somber.

Azlan nodded slightly, the weight of the situation sinking in even further. More tears silently slid down his face, mingling with the sweat on his pillow.

Azlan took a deep breath, his voice barely audible as he asked, "How long have I been out?"

"Almost a day now," Abraham answered, glancing out the window. The bright red sky hinted that the storm had passed, with dusk slowly approaching.

Abraham's phone buzzed again. He quickly answered, "I'll call you later," and hung up.

"Who was it? Could be important," Azlan murmured weakly, hinting that he didn't want Abraham missing anything on his account.

"It was just Irene," Abraham said, slipping his phone back into his pocket. "I'll call her later. She's probably checking in because of the attack."

"She doesn't care about me, huh?" Azlan chuckled weakly, attempting to distract himself from the pain, but it was clear his humor failed as the sorrow remained etched on his face.

Abraham sighed. "I guess she doesn't know about your condition yet. I haven't spoken to her since..." He trailed off, unsure how to finish his sentence, the weight of Azlan's condition making the words stick in his throat.

The room fell into a heavy silence once again, the weight of unspoken emotions pressing down on both of them. The rhythmic beeping of the machines and the faint sound of the hospital beyond the walls were the only interruptions.

Then, Abraham's phone buzzed again. He glanced at the screen, his brow furrowing in clear annoyance. He sighed, pocketing the phone, determined to stay by Azlan's side.

Azlan noticed the hesitation and gave a slight nod, his voice barely audible. "You should take it."

Abraham shifted uncomfortably. "It's just Irene again."

Azlan managed a faint smile, though sorrow still lingered in his eyes. "She's probably been trying... it could be important."

Abraham looked uncertain but nodded. "I won't be long." He gave Azlan's hand a final squeeze before releasing it and turning toward the door.

As he walked out, he threw one last glance over his shoulder, his expression a mix of concern and reluctance. The door clicked shut behind him, leaving Azlan alone in the sterile quiet.

For a moment, Azlan lay there, staring at the ceiling, his mind numb and his heart heavy. The emptiness of the room mirrored the hollowness inside him.

He took a shuddering breath, his chest aching with the weight of loss.

The sound of footsteps echoed faintly from the hallway, but in this moment, it was just him and the suffocating grief.

..

11 HUMILITY

Recognizing and accepting one's limitations and flaws, valuing others' contributions, and maintaining a modest and respectful attitude, which fosters cooperation, learning, and personal growth, and strengthens community bonds.

"Do you have any idea what's going on here? Don't you think if I hang up, I'll call you back?" Abraham shouted into the phone, his voice cutting through the noise of the traffic.

He was standing in the designated smoking area in front of the hospital, frustration evident in his tone. A few heads turned in his direction, startled by his outburst.

Realizing how harsh he sounded, Abraham took a deep breath, trying to compose himself.

"Sorry," he muttered. "I'm in a difficult situation right now. You remember Azlan?"

"Of course I do. How could I forget your best friend?" Irene responded, concern mixed with a hint of urgency in her voice.

"He and his family were caught in the bomb blast yesterday. His wife and daughter didn't make it, and he's badly injured. He just woke up when you were calling, and it's been... really emotional. That's why I couldn't pick up." He paused, letting the weight of his words settle before adding, "So, how are you?"

"Not great," Irene replied, jumping right to the point. It wasn't that she wasn't affected by what happened to Azlan, but the urgency in her own situation couldn't be ignored. "I need your help."

Abraham remained silent, waiting for Irene to explain what she needed. He was confident he could help—after all, he'd never failed her before. Whether it was buying her lunch or beating up the guy who used to stalk her, Abraham had always been there when she asked. But he had a strict principle—he only helped when someone explicitly asked for it. To him, if someone was too proud to ask for help, they didn't deserve it. Abraham wouldn't intervene unless a person had done everything they could to solve their problem on their own. But once you reached that point, you could count on him without fail. And Irene knew that better than anyone else.

"I need you to send me one ton of rice," she said softly.

"One ton? As in a thousand kilograms of rice?" Abraham repeated, surprise flooding his voice. The request seemed strange, especially coming from Irene, who always boasted that her village was the best at growing rice.

"Why? Did one of your experiments go wrong and ruin your harvest?" he teased, trying to lighten the mood.

Irene stayed silent for a few moments.

"I'm in big trouble. I need one ton of rice before Wednesday," she began, the urgency clear in her tone.

"Wednesday? That's in three days! Even if I could get it, transport, customs—it's impossible. Why didn't you reach out to me earlier?" Abraham's voice rose, not in frustration, but in genuine concern that this time, he might not be able to help her.

Irene quickly explained what had happened. Abraham understood the gravity of her situation. He knew very well that she would sacrifice herself before putting her village in trouble.

His mind quickly started thinking of ways he could help her.

"I have an idea, but it means you have to do something

else on top of what I already asked of you," Irene gently interrupted his thoughts.

"Tell me. I'll do it if I can," Abraham assured her.

"I need you to contact Inara."

"Inara? No. But why?" Abraham asked.

"To get information on how PeTiTe works. Because you need to teleport the rice to me. Normal routes won't work. Ayden will find a way to stop it from reaching me."

Abraham remained silent. His sudden silence was something Irene couldn't quite read.

"I can build one here, and you one there. We'll teleport the rice through this. It's critical. More important than just securing the rice. I know a farmer who lives not far from you. I've spoken to him already. He'll deliver the rice to you tomorrow…"

"Wait, you already have the rice?" Abraham interjected, surprised.

"Yes. I asked you to send it, not buy it. Is my English unclear to you?" Irene replied, her tone a mix of frustration and humor, not really expecting an answer.

Abraham let out a small chuckle, appreciating her sarcasm even in the midst of her difficult situation.

"And this guy will bring some of his trusted men to help pack it into a thousand packages. Trust me, I've tried every other option. I really need your help to teleport it," Irene continued, her voice now soft but laced with urgency, hoping Abraham would understand how serious this was.

"It's not that…" Abraham hesitated.

"Come on! Stub your ego in the ashtray and talk to Inara. She's ambitious, not evil. She'll understand my situation and help. The fate of my whole village depends on this. My fate depends on this," Irene pleaded, trying to appeal to Abraham's better nature.

"It's not that I don't want to talk to Inara. I'd take any excuse to talk to her."

"Then what's the problem?" Irene asked, confused.

"I already know how it works. In fact, I'm the one who shared the key insight with Inara. Well, indirectly. I gave her the solution so subtly, she didn't even realize it came from me."

"Yes, yes. You're noble. You're a gentleman. You still love her," Irene teased, feeling relieved now that she realized Abraham would be able to help. "So, how do we do this? Video call? You'll guide me in building it? It would be better if we finish it before the rice even reaches you."

A smile crept onto Abraham's face for two reasons. First, he was glad to hear Irene relax and slip back into her usual self. Second, he had a better plan forming in his mind.

"Tell your guy to hold on. Let's have a call in three hours, and you be ready in your workshop," Abraham told her with confidence.

Irene simply nodded, though she knew Abraham couldn't see her, and hung up, wondering what trick he had up his sleeve this time.

12 GLUTTONY

*Excessive indulgence and consumption of food or drink,
reflecting a lack of self-control and an insatiable appetite that
disregards health and the needs of others, leading to physical
and spiritual detriment.*

"Azlan? Dude?"

Abraham called out as he entered Azlan's apartment, using the spare key he had. In one hand, he held a takeout package that smelled like food.

The apartment was shrouded in darkness, despite it being noon, with heavy curtains drawn over the windows, blocking out all natural light. The air was thick with a pungent smell, a sign that the place hadn't been aired out in days. Even in the dim light, Abraham could see the chaos—dishes piled up, clothes strewn across the floor, and a general sense of neglect hanging over the room.

On the couch, Azlan sat slumped in the corner, staring off into space, lost in thought. He wore the same pajamas he'd been in since leaving the hospital almost a week ago. His beard had grown scruffy, a clear sign he hadn't shaved, and the stains on his clothes, combined with the stale smell that clung to him, suggested he hadn't showered either.

"Azlan? You eaten lunch?" Abraham asked calmly as he walked closer, ignoring the mess and focusing on his friend's state.

Azlan didn't respond. He continued to stare blankly at the TV, which was turned off.

Abraham found a clear spot on the dining table and set down the takeout package. Without a word, he went over to the windows, pulling the curtains open and cracking the windows and balcony door to let in some fresh air. The sudden flood of light made Azlan squint, and the cool breeze prickled his skin, causing him to shift uncomfortably on the couch. His eyes slowly followed Abraham as he moved around the room.

"Go take a shower and get ready. I brought biryani," Abraham said, his tone casual, as he started picking up trash and clearing the floor.

Azlan ignored the suggestion, still seated, watching Abraham tidying up but making no move to help.

"Up!" Abraham ordered firmly, as he picked up the throw pillows and began beating them to rid them of dust. Azlan, though slow to react, finally stood and shuffled away from the couch, his movements stiff and disoriented.

Noticing Azlan's hesitation, Abraham quickly passed him on the way to the bedroom, returning with a towel. He handed it to Azlan and gently steered him toward the bathroom.

Once Abraham heard the water running, he resumed tidying up the living room, clearing the trash and organizing the space. By the time Azlan returned, his hair still damp, the apartment felt less suffocating, the windows letting in a fresh breeze.

"Let's eat," Abraham said, unpacking the biryani onto the now-cleared dining table. He motioned for Azlan to join him, but Azlan hesitated before sitting down across from him. His eyes were on Abraham, filled with questions he wasn't ready to voice.

As they began eating in silence, Azlan couldn't hold it in any longer.

"You disappeared," he said, his voice strained but controlled. "I haven't heard from you since the hospital.

What happened? Why now?"

Abraham paused mid-bite, his eyes fixed on the plate. He expected this. "I had to handle some things, man," he replied, avoiding eye contact. His voice was steady, but there was a careful distance in it.

"Handle things?" Azlan repeated, his frustration bubbling to the surface. "What's that supposed to mean?"

Abraham exhaled, continuing to eat slowly. "I'll explain later, man. Right now, let's just focus on getting you back on your feet."

Azlan quietly nibbled through his food, his appetite weak. Abraham, eating at his usual pace, had already finished half his plate while Azlan had barely made a dent in his.

After a pause, Abraham continued, "Irene had an issue and asked for help. It was time-sensitive, so I had to be there for her."

Azlan's frustration wavered, replaced by concern. "Oh no. What happened?"

He knew that if Irene reached out to Abraham for help, it had to be serious. Abraham wasn't one to jump in unless it was really necessary.

"That guy who runs the province—Ayden," Abraham clarified, "he did something to her village. Forced them to pay a penalty in the form of a ton of rice. If they didn't, Irene would have to serve as a sort of... slave for a year."

Azlan, distracted now by the unfolding story, leaned in slightly, intrigued.

"Did you manage to get her the rice?" Azlan asked.

"That wasn't the problem," Abraham replied. "She had the rice already lined up."

"Then why did she need you?" Azlan pressed, though his voice remained weak.

"Well, she needed help getting it into her village. Ayden's men were patrolling the border, waiting to stop it. So, she needed a less... conventional route." Abraham explained.

"Smuggling a thousand kilograms of rice? Did you manage to pull it off?" Azlan's curiosity deepened, the story drawing him out of his haze.

Abraham gave a small smile. "Yeah, I did."

Azlan, despite his earlier anger, couldn't help but feel proud. His friend had once again proven he could go to any lengths to help someone in need. The frustration from before seemed to melt away, replaced by a sense of quiet admiration.

Azlan had eaten more than he realized, the food easing the weight he'd been carrying. "So, how'd you manage to smuggle it?" he asked, genuinely interested now.

Abraham grinned, leaning back in his chair. "I'll tell you, but only after you finish that biryani."

Azlan focused on his food, trying his best to finish it. Meanwhile, Abraham, having already cleared his own plate, stood up and went to the kitchen. He returned with a bottle of multivitamin juice and two glasses, placing them on the table before collecting Azlan's empty plate. As Abraham placed the plate in the dishwasher, Azlan washed his hands and returned to his seat.

When he sat back down, Abraham poured the juice into the glasses and handed one to Azlan. "Well," Abraham began with a smile, "I invented something and solved her problem."

Azlan raised an eyebrow, intrigued. "I thought Inara invented teleportation. How could you invent something that's already been invented?" He seemed eager to challenge Abraham, sensing there was more to the story.

Abraham chuckled. "Why is teleportation everyone's go-to solution? Irene said the same thing," he mused, remembering his conversation with her. "And no, I'm not about to take credit for that. Teleportation is Inara's baby, through and through," Abraham assured him, deliberately holding back the fact that he had indirectly helped Inara with the solution—something he'd revealed too carelessly to Irene.

Azlan's curiosity deepened. "So, what exactly did you invent?"

Enjoying his friend's intrigue, Abraham leaned in, savoring the moment. "Time travel!" he exclaimed, his eyes wide, his hands gesturing dramatically as if telling a fantastical tale.

Azlan stared at him, a mix of disbelief and wonder on his face. He knew time travel was theoretically possible, but he hadn't expected it to come so soon. Still, he couldn't quite connect the dots. "How did time travel help Irene? You went back in time and... what? Killed Ayden?"

Abraham grinned, not wanting to diminish Azlan's excitement. He scooted closer, ready to explain. "No, nothing that extreme," he said. "But let me ask you this: What happens when you travel back in time? Say you go back by one hour—how many Azlans would there be?"

"Two," Azlan replied, quick on the uptake but still unsure where this was going.

"Exactly," Abraham said, his excitement building. "Now, say the second Azlan goes and joins the first Azlan after another hour, and they both travel back in time again. How many Azlans then?"

Azlan thought for a moment. "Four?"

"Precisely!" Abraham's enthusiasm was contagious. "Do that a few more times and you get exponential growth. It's like that old story about the inventor of chess and the grains of rice. Remember?"

Azlan nodded, though his curiosity deepened. "But wouldn't that break what we know about quantum physics and time travel? Shouldn't they exist in parallel universes? If I travel back in time, shouldn't I stop existing in this timeline from that point onward? Wouldn't all those 'extra' versions of me only exist for that one-hour gap? And after the final one travels back, wouldn't only that version be left?"

Abraham grinned at the depth of Azlan's questions, thrilled that his friend was fully engaged in the topic. "Yes, exactly. But here's the twist—what if, after all that time traveling, the last group decided not to travel back again? They'd keep existing, wouldn't they?"

Azlan leaned back, thoughtful, trying to wrap his mind around it. "Yeah, but... I feel like I'm missing something here."

"Well, when I was decoding qDNA information, we were

able to easily identify the positional data because the rate of change in the information aligned perfectly with the Earth's rotation speed. So, PeTiTe works by using two machines that measure the differences in x, y, and z coordinates between them, and then it feeds that data into a process that manipulates space information at the qDNA level," Abraham explained, his voice growing more animated.

But Azlan seemed lost in thought, barely paying attention to the explanation.

Abraham continued, trying to get his friend's attention. "While I was working on this, I also isolated a specific sequence in qDNA that corresponds to the object's position in time. It didn't reflect its age, but the time in which it exists. I noticed that this particular sequence in qDNA was the same in all objects. It's like a timestamp that reflects the moment an object exists in, regardless of how old it is. But that was key in figuring out how to manipulate objects across different points in time, not just space."

Abraham kept talking, hoping to draw Azlan back into the conversation.

"So, you're saying you can time travel?" Azlan asked, as if he had ignored everything else Abraham had been explaining.

"Yes, and I wrote a code that will stop after certain cycles. So, Irene was able to get all the rice she needed without help from anybody. Thinking of which, I think we can end the resource problem on Earth now," Abraham continued, smiling with enthusiasm.

"So, I can save Ieasha?" Azlan asked calmly.

Abraham's excitement stopped suddenly, and a deep worry began to grow as he realized what he might have started.

13 TEMPERANCE

Practicing self-restraint and moderation in all aspects of life, particularly in consumption and desires, to achieve balance and harmony, and to prevent overindulgence that can lead to harm and discontent.

"No, it doesn't work like that. It's… it's very complicated," Abraham stammered, struggling to find the right words.

"Why not? I saw in the news where the terrorists assembled the bomb, when they left their place—everything. All I need to do is send a petrol bomb to their hideout a few minutes before they leave. I can stop the bombing from happening at all," Azlan said, his mind already formulating a plan.

Abraham's heart sank. "It's not that easy, Azlan," he said quietly. "Time travel is extremely complicated. I told you about the Earth's rotation already. But it's more than that. We have to account for the Earth's revolution around the sun, the movement of our solar system, and so much more. The Earth rotates at about 460 meters per second, and we orbit the sun at 30 kilometers per second. If you miscalculate by even a microscopic fraction, you'll end up placing the object completely off target. For Irene, I had to move grains of rice back in time by mere nanoseconds—actually, much less than that to avoid issues with Earth's movement. And you're talking about sending something back a whole week. It's… impossible."

Abraham stopped, his breath ragged, but Azlan's gaze remained steady, fixed on him. His face held a calmness that contrasted with the slight shimmer in his eyes, suggesting an unspoken depth beneath the surface. He didn't shift, didn't blink, just watched.

"It's not possible, man!" Abraham repeated, his voice edged with a desperate plea, as if he were trying to convince both Azlan and himself.

"You've already solved it, haven't you?" Azlan's voice was soft, but resolute. His eyes, though glistening with unshed tears, didn't waver. He remained still, his words carrying a quiet confidence, something unspoken in the way his gaze lingered on Abraham.

Abraham froze, his mind scrambling for an answer. "What? What are you talking about?" he stammered, the words feeling hollow as they left his mouth.

"I have faint memories, fragments, of two versions of you," Azlan continued, his tone steady despite the tears now threatening to break through. "I'm sure both of them happened. Based on what you've said, it doesn't seem like there's an alternate universe. The three-dimensional universe has its parallel along the fourth dimension—time. So, all that talk about alternate or parallel universes... it's wrong. Any changes made to the past affect the present. We live through the consequences, but we retain the other version—like a memory, a dream... a lucid dream."

Abraham sat in stunned silence, his pulse racing.

"That's why I remember you differently. It's why I have these memories of you being chaste when you were actually a playboy. I couldn't explain it before, but now I know—you've altered your past, haven't you?"

Though his eyes were misty, Azlan's voice remained firm, leaving the question hanging, waiting.

"Yes." Abraham sighed, realizing he could no longer hide the truth. "Yes, I wrote a code that accounts for the Earth's rotation, the movement of the solar system—every motion that affects our position as much as possible. When I specify a point on Earth and the time I want to be there, it makes the necessary coordinate corrections. So no, we didn't have to send the grains back in nanoseconds because my code handled the problem."

He finally confessed, unable to lie to his best friend any longer—especially now that Azlan had almost pieced everything together.

"Then help me save Ieasha. Our Ieasha," Azlan pleaded, his voice barely above a whisper as he grasped Abraham's hands. "Your goddaughter."

Abraham sat frozen, searching for the right words to explain the dangers.

"You're right. I changed my past," he began slowly. "After helping Irene—which was on Wednesday—I got selfish. I wanted to use it to save my relationship with Inara. To avoid altering reality too much, I tried to change the latest possible point—the call. I thought maybe she wasn't trying to break up with me. Maybe if I'd listened, been patient, things would have been different. We could have been together."

Thinking about the past stirred emotions he'd tried to suppress. Not one to surrender to his feelings, he paused and poured himself another glass of juice, taking a sip to soothe his tightening throat.

Azlan remained silent, waiting for him to continue.

"So, I wrote myself a note: 'Listen to her during the call and don't interrupt her.' You know what happened after I read the note?" Abraham looked up.

"Yes—nothing. You behaved the same way you always did. People don't change, blah, blah," Azlan replied bluntly. "I remember from our conversation. So you're saying no matter what I do, I can't change the past? I can't bring back Ieasha?"

"No. That small note changed the decisions I made afterward. Instead of being heartbroken and avoiding relationships with lame excuses, I became a heartbroken jerk who went around sleeping with any girl I could."

"So you're saying changing the past will change me? An

asshole like you? I don't care, as long as I save Ieasha."

"No!" Abraham snapped, his frustration spilling over. He took a deep breath, trying to calm himself. "Remember the headaches we got?"

Azlan nodded silently, not wanting to interrupt.

"You had a headache from just seeing a different version of your life that lasted less than an hour. Now imagine the girls I spent whole nights with—days, even. Think about the impact on their lives. Stella was supposed to visit her mom, who was in the hospital for chemo. But I was selfish. I pretended to care, offered to drive her so she could stay late at the office to finish her project. We were alone, and... well, you can guess what happened. She missed the chance to be with her mom."

Azlan remained unfazed. "So what? She got a headache? I can deal with that if it means I save Ieasha."

Abraham hesitated, then spoke softly. "No, Azlan. Her mom died." His voice wavered. "Her mom went hysterical, thinking Stella had been there, that she'd slept in the same room. The doctors said it was just hallucinations, a side effect of the treatment. But everything was wrong—different from what should've happened. Her mind was holding onto the altered reality—one where Stella had visited her, creating a conflict between memories from different timelines. The clash between what she believed and what actually happened confused her mind, and she couldn't handle the stress. Her body gave out. Do you know how long it took? Just twenty-five minutes."

Azlan listened, though it wasn't clear if he grasped the gravity of what Abraham was saying. "But Ieasha would be alive."

"Ripple effect, man! Butterfly effect!" Abraham shouted, his voice rising in urgency. "You kill those five terrorists, sure—you save thousands from that bombing. But what happens after that? Those thousands go on to touch millions of lives. And it doesn't stop there. Say one of the saved ends up becoming a serial killer—someone who wasn't even involved in the bombing in the first place. He kills people who were never part of this chain of events, and suddenly, you've created a whole new timeline. A branch off of this alternate reality, spiraling further and further from the original."

Abraham paused, his expression tightening. "Each new branch? It brings more people into it. People who were never supposed to live, now dragging others along with them. Their minds would be filled with fragmented memories of alternate lives—things that never happened. Their brains won't be able to handle it. It's not just about saving thousands anymore—you're risking the deaths of millions in ways you can't even imagine. Do you really want that on your conscience?"

"If Ieasha survives..." Azlan answered, his voice calm and unwavering, his eyes still brimming with unshed tears.

Abraham stared hard at him, searching his face for some flicker of doubt. But Azlan's gaze stayed steady, resolute, unflinching in the face of everything Abraham had said.

Without another word, Abraham abruptly stood up and stormed out of the apartment. Azlan's gaze drifted toward the door that had slammed shut behind him. His hand, now resting on the table, absentmindedly rolled the empty glass. The glass, like his mind, felt hollow—void of purpose, spinning in endless circles, mirroring the emptiness within.

Minutes passed in silence after Abraham had stormed out, but then the door swung open once again. Abraham re-entered the apartment, his face tight with resolve. Without a word, he threw a small PeTiTe device onto the floor in front of Azlan, the metallic object clattering between them.

"You want to play god? Fine," Abraham growled, marching across the room to the cabinet where Azlan kept his stash of alcohol and old rags. He yanked a bottle of whiskey out, along with some tattered cloth. "Here's your chance. If you think saving Ieasha, and risking the lives of millions, is the way forward—then go ahead." He tossed the rags onto the table in front of Azlan, his eyes blazing. "Make your bomb. Kill the terrorists."

Azlan sat quietly for a moment, the device lying between

them like some twisted symbol of fate. His fingers moved slowly, methodically, as he began tearing the rags, soaking them in alcohol with practiced precision. "Ieasha has a chance," Azlan murmured, his voice steady yet weighed down with emotion. His hands worked steadily as he built the crude petrol bomb. The lighter flicked, its tiny flame sparking in the dim light.

Abraham stood frozen in disbelief as Azlan calmly went about his task, the fire licking at the rag now stuffed into the neck of the alcohol bottle.

He's bluffing, Abraham thought, a flicker of doubt creeping in. Azlan will come to his senses before he goes through with it, right? Abraham stormed toward the PeTiTe device, swiftly adjusting the coordinates and time settings with angry precision. "Fine. By this setting, the bottle will drop from the ceiling directly over the terrorists. You press that button, Azlan, and it's done. They're dead."

Azlan's hand hovered over the device, his face unreadable, but there was no hesitation in his eyes.

Before Abraham could react, Azlan's fingers pressed the "Go" button.

The bottle, aflame and deadly, vanished.

A silence hung thick in the air between them. Abraham's heart raced, his mind swirling with disbelief and fear of what had just transpired.

Suddenly, the shrill ring of a phone cut through the tension. Azlan's phone lit up on the table, its screen flashing the name: Irem. His wife.

For a second, neither of them moved. Then, Azlan's hand, trembling, reached for the phone. He answered, pressing it slowly to his ear, his breath shallow.

"Irem?" he whispered.

The voice on the other end was frantic. "Where the hell are you?" she screamed, the panic in her voice unmistakable. "Ieasha and I have been waiting at the ice cream shop for 30 minutes! You were supposed to pick us up!"

Azlan's face crumpled, tears spilling freely down his cheeks as a smile, wide and joyous, tugged at his lips. His hands shook as he clutched the phone tighter, laughter mixing with his tears. "I-Irem... Ieasha..."

But as the moment of euphoria washed over him, blood began to trickle from his nose, a small crimson stream snaking its way down his upper lip. His grip on the phone loosened as his smile faltered. The overload was beginning.

The glass in his other hand rolled off the table, hitting the floor with a dull thud, as Azlan's eyes filled with happiness—and a looming shadow of what was to come.

IGNORANCE

The café was abandoned, its once-bustling interior now silent and lifeless. Tables stood empty, chairs pushed aside as though the last customers had left in a hurry. Dust had begun to settle on the countertops, and the faint smell of stale coffee lingered in the air. No one worked here anymore. No one worked anywhere. There was no point. The world had stopped caring.

Adrien and Andre sat in the corner by the window, their eyes fixed on the horizon. The Moon hung low in the sky, much larger than it had been just days ago. Its surface was eerily detailed, the craters and ridges visible even to the naked eye. The unnatural closeness made it feel like a predator, waiting to strike. The air was thick with an oppressive tension that neither man had the words to articulate.

"Hard to believe it's come to this," Adrien muttered, his voice barely above a whisper. His fingers traced idle patterns on the dusty table. "The Moon… it looks like it's ready to swallow us whole."

Andre said nothing for a long moment. His gaze remained fixed on the sky, where the Moon loomed like a terrible omen. "It's getting closer every day," he said finally, his voice hollow. "Nothing left to do but wait."

Adrien glanced around the empty café, the desolation weighing on him. "I guess no one cares to show up for work when the world's ending."

Andre allowed a faint, humorless chuckle. "What's the point in making coffee when you can spend your last moments with your loved ones?"

They sat in silence for a while, the stillness of the café amplifying the distant, almost imperceptible tremors beneath their feet. Everyone knew what was coming now. The Moon's slow, inexorable descent toward Earth was no longer just a scientific prediction—it was a death sentence. Days. That's all they had left.

"I still can't wrap my head around it," Adrien said, shaking his head as if trying to clear the fog of disbelief. "India and China… They were just trying to end the resource crisis. The PeTiTe device was supposed to save us."

Andre leaned forward, resting his elbows on the table. His eyes were dark, distant. "No one could have predicted this. They wanted to solve the greatest problem of our time—end hunger, poverty, scarcity. The governments believed they were doing the right thing, Adrien. Using PeTiTe to produce more resources seemed like a miracle. But…"

"But they should have controlled it," Adrien finished for him, his voice quiet, as if speaking the truth out loud made it worse. "Too much mass, too fast. And now the Moon's falling on us."

Andre nodded slowly. "Yeah. And then, after that, we'll be consumed by the Sun. Luckily, we won't be alive to feel the wrath of the Sun. Nobody thought that a device so small could bring about something like this. The more mass they created, the more it threw everything out of balance."

Adrien stared at the Moon, his chest tight with fear. "What about nuking it? Destroy PeTiTe. Couldn't that stop it?"

Andre's expression didn't change. "And what if it multiplies the effect of the nuke? If PeTiTe's still active when the blast hits, we're not just looking at a device destroyed. We're looking at the entire Earth being torn apart. There's no guarantee the explosion wouldn't cascade into something far worse. That's why they decided not to. But now it's too late to reconsider."

Adrien leaned back in his chair, the weight of the situation settling in like a cold stone in his gut. "So, we just… wait?"

Andre sighed deeply. "That's all anyone can do now. There's no fixing this. The damage was done."

The Moon seemed to loom closer with every passing minute, its pale glow casting long shadows over the deserted streets outside the café. In the distance, a group of people had gathered, staring up at the sky as though hoping for some last-minute miracle. But no miracle was coming.

"We really thought we were doing the right thing," Adrien whispered, more to himself than to Andre. "It was supposed to make the world better."

Andre's gaze flickered toward him, his expression unreadable. "We were ignorant," he said quietly. "We didn't know what we were unleashing. None of us did."

Silence stretched between them, heavy and suffocating. The wind outside picked up, rattling the windows of the café, and for a moment, the low rumble of the Earth's shifting crust could be heard—a reminder that the end was not only inevitable but near.

Adrien stared at the Moon, its massive form dominating the sky. "It feels wrong to just sit here. To not try something."

Andre's voice was low but steady. "There's nothing left to try. All we can do is accept it. At least it will bring peace."

Adrien didn't respond. He knew Andre was right, but the knowledge brought no comfort. The Moon, once a symbol of mystery and wonder, was now a harbinger of death, pulling ever closer, its gravitational force growing stronger by the hour.

The two men sat in the abandoned café, watching as the world they knew crumbled under the weight of its own ambition. The end was inevitable. No amount of regret or self-recrimination could change that.

The silence between them grew heavier, mirroring the quiet resignation that had settled over the world. And as the Moon loomed overhead, casting its eerie light over the dying Earth, they sat and waited for the inevitable collision—the moment when ignorance would finally be paid in full.

14 KINDNESS

Exhibiting compassion, empathy, and consideration in interactions with others, actively seeking to promote their well-being and happiness, and creating a positive and supportive environment through gentle and caring actions.

Austin was enjoying the freshness of his body, clad only in his boxers, as he sat in front of his computer in the laboratory downstairs. Behind him, the operating table held Anton, unconscious and stripped naked, his wound now tended to. A bandage was wrapped tightly around his waist. A small patch of blood stained the right side of the bandage where he had been shot, and there was a similar patch of blood on the left side of his hip as well.

Ivanna descended the stairs gracefully, a light cover wrapped around her. She approached Austin from behind, her hand brushing his shoulder, her voice close to his ear, a gentle warmth in her breath. Austin felt a chill run through his body, a smile creeping across his lips.

"What are you doing?" Ivanna whispered, her Russian accent thicker and more alluring than ever.

"I'm trying to save your boyfriend," Austin replied, his eyes still fixed on the computer screen, typing what appeared to be a complex code. A faint grin flickered when he said "boyfriend."

"I didn't know you could patch up a bullet wound with a computer program. I thought you had to patch it up manually," Ivanna responded playfully, shifting to sit on the table facing Austin. She gently rubbed his arm, teasingly.

"No, we still need to patch him up manually," Austin explained. "The bullet tore through his right kidney. What I'm doing here is duplicating his left kidney using time travel, so he'll have two healthy kidneys."

"What?" Ivanna asked, her curiosity piqued as she turned her gaze to the screen. "Is that even possible? I've heard about teleportation, but I thought we couldn't teleport living things. And time travel? I heard the pandemic was caused by time travel. I don't understand... maybe you can teach me." Her voice carried a teasing edge, as though inviting him into a game.

"Well, it's about manipulating information at the quantum level, much smaller than atoms." Austin tried to explain, and Ivanna nodded playfully, pretending to understand.

"You get more attractive when you talk science," she murmured, running her fingers along his chin.

"There was a girl at my university in the physics department who invented teleportation. Inara," he recalled.

"I bet you did her too. You're such a charismatic man," Ivanna teased.

"No. She was a fatty. I get turned off by those types. Actually annoyed. She wanted to join my lectures in molecular biology, but her presence itself annoyed me. I had to kick her out."

"You're losing my interest. Stick to the science," Ivanna interrupted, placing a finger on his lips.

Austin pretended to bite her finger playfully and continued. "The teleportation was initially successful for non-living objects, which don't have memory. Or memory that is different. But living things are different. They couldn't identify the right quantum code for living tissues. That's where I come in. I'm a genius when it comes to biology." He pointed to the screen, expecting to impress her. "See this part of the code? This is specific to living cells. I'm writing a program that will allow living cells to teleport and even time travel."

"This one?" Ivanna asked, feigning interest, as her finger traced over the screen, resting her other hand on the back of Austin. As her eyes scanned the lines of code, her body began to tremble. Her hands started to shake, and Austin noticed the shift, turning to look at her in confusion.

"I need a drink," she blurted suddenly, pushing away from the table and heading to the bar. "Should I pour one for you too?"

"Sure. Whiskey. Neat. From the one on the third shelf from the top," Austin replied, eyeing her curiously, wondering why she was suddenly behaving differently.

Ivanna stood by the bar, breathing deeply for a minute before grabbing two glasses. She poured whiskey into both and returned to Austin, handing him one.

Ivanna settled herself back onto the desk, the draped fabric shifting slightly with her movements. She clinked glasses with Austin and downed her drink in one gulp. Austin took a sip, watching her with growing confusion.

Ivanna swiftly placed one leg on the chair between Austin's legs and leaned toward him.

"Can I tell you a secret?" she whispered, her breath brushing his ear as she leaned in closer.

Austin's heart raced, her sudden intimacy sending waves of excitement through him. He nodded, eager to hear more.

"I'm actually pretty smart too," she said, placing her hands on his shoulders, the sheet held loosely around her.

Austin's eyes flickered down instinctively, momentarily distracted by the sight. His pulse quickened, and for a brief second, his thoughts drifted. But before he could fully lose himself, Ivanna's voice cut through, sharp and cold, pulling his attention back.

"You know, after you insulted me and kicked me out of your class, I set a goal for myself: to become the kind of woman you fantasize about. Not to impress you—just to prove that anyone could be what you idealize. But as we made progress on teleportation in qAI, I knew you'd be the one to crack the code for living tissue. Still, I couldn't simply come to you for help. You're an egotistical, self-absorbed, narcissistic bastard. And yes, I also hate you."

Austin's face paled as the situation began to dawn on him. A cold sweat broke out, despite the air-conditioned room.

"I hired this guy to act hurt, but he backed out at the last minute because he realized he actually had to get hurt. Got scared, I guess. Even though I paid him a million. So I had to shoot him and break his trachea so he wouldn't talk. Didn't you notice how he was bruised all over, while I showed up without a single scratch? Ah, you were too busy admiring my body, weren't you?"

"But… you? How?" Austin stammered, his voice shaky.

"Shhh," Ivanna pressed a firm finger to his lips, silencing him. "You were so mesmerized by my exposed body, you couldn't even tell my Indian face from Russian. You didn't care, did you? Just a cheap, perverted little man—that's all you are."

Austin's mind struggled to process the shift, his confidence fading under her cold, unyielding stare. A chill washed over him as he realized the danger he was in.

"Do you know what my superpower is? I don't just learn like other people do. When I study, I feel it. I understand it with every fiber of my being. Watch this." She lifted her finger from his lips and stared at it. Slowly, her perfect index finger began to elongate and transform, shimmering like metal until it became a thin, sharp needle.

"See? I visualized it, and now I've altered the information of my finger at the quantum level." She smiled wickedly, watching Austin's horrified expression. "It is a weapon now."

"I feel unstoppable, like I've tapped into limitless power. I can do anything." Ivanna shrugged her whole body as if she were a little girl excited by the sight of a unicorn.

"Let's see if I can put it to good use," she whispered, before driving the needle-like finger into Austin's wide, disbelieving eye.

Austin didn't scream. His body convulsed violently, limbs thrashing as if trying to resist, but no sound escaped his lips.

The needle had found its mark deep within his brain, and whatever reaction he might have had was trapped, silenced by the damage. Slowly, the violent shaking subsided, until his body finally lay still.

She withdrew her finger and watched it morph back to its original form.

Rising from the table, Ivanna glanced down, and with a thought, her ripped jeans and vest materialized out of thin air, covering her instantly. Her boots reformed around her feet as she stepped away from the table. She turned to Anton, lying unconscious, his chest rising and falling in shallow breaths.

She walked closer to him, staring intently. Focusing intently, she manipulated his tissues at the quantum level. Like magic, the torn flesh knitted together, and his broken trachea aligned, allowing him to take a full, deep breath. His eyes fluttered open, confusion filling them as he looked around, recalling only the moment he was shot. Slowly, he touched his side, surprised to feel no pain, and attempted to speak, his voice faint. "What… happened?"

Ivanna held his gaze for a brief moment, then gave a subtle nod, signaling him to leave. Still bewildered, he managed a shaky, "Thank you," before rising unsteadily to his feet and limping toward the exit, casting one last look of confusion over his shoulder.

Ivanna watched him go, her expression unreadable. Then, as her gaze shifted, her focus turned cold. She walked over to the bar, methodically tossing bottles of alcohol across the lab, glass shattering with each throw. As she reached the stairs, she paused, casting one last, deliberate glance at the room. The alcohol ignited instantly, flames spreading in a slow, deliberate crawl, as if obeying her silent command. Satisfied, she turned and ascended the stairs, leaving the fire to consume the lab behind her.

A smile crept across her lips as she exited the room.

A NEW STORY BEGINS

The dishes had been cleaned, dried, and neatly stacked away. The kitchen was quiet, save for the soft hiss of batter spreading on the hot pan. Anu stood by the stove, expertly crafting dosa after dosa, the thin, golden edges crisping up perfectly. Next to him, perched casually on the kitchen counter, Inara sat with a plate in hand, waiting for Anu to prepare the next dosa and serve her.

Anu, his focus drifting away from the dosa for a moment as the weight of the story settled in, asked, "So… the Earth is destroyed, and no one survived?"

"Yes, I guess so," Inara replied casually, licking her finger as she savored the spicy tomato chutney.

"And you were posing as Ivanna and gained the knowledge of manipulating... How do you say that again?" Anu's curiosity broke through.

"Quantum DNA," Inara responded, just as casually. "And that's how I can manipulate my body. Not just that—my body instinctively transforms to protect me from any damage."

To demonstrate, Inara placed her hand directly over the flames of the stove. Instinctively, her hand shifted into a metallic-like material, reflecting the light from the fire. As she pulled her hand away, it seamlessly transformed back into its normal, human appearance, as though nothing had happened.

Anu took the sizzling dosa and served it to Inara. Her display of tricks didn't amuse him anymore—it just gave him more clarity.

"And I guess your body instinctively teleported you to this Earth when your world was being destroyed?" Anu asked, as he poured the batter onto the pan for the next dosa.

"See, that's why I came to you. You learn quickly," Inara said, maintaining her casual cheer. "Teleported to this Earth, or time traveled to a different time on the same Earth, or a parallel universe—I don't really know." She shrugged, taking another bite.

"My self-awareness and instinct to survive have reached such a level that I don't even make conscious decisions anymore. As a matter of fact, I can't die, not even if I want to. Even when I tried... my body just rejected it and kept me alive," she said, continuing to enjoy the freshly made dosa as if she were discussing something as casual as the weather.

"So, you're an immortal? How long have you been roaming around on this Earth?"

"You don't want to know that," she replied, her tone hinting at something far deeper. She wasn't ready to deviate from her objective.

Anu flipped the dosa, thinking over her response as if he had understood the hint.

"You said you wanted my help. What is it? You want me to write a book about your story? It would be a bestseller fiction novel, and you could make a lot of money. I could make some money as well," he said, fishing for her true intent.

"What all your fiction stories show is that an immortal like me always maintains a low profile. Well, that's been true in my case as well. I've kept a low profile for ages now. But lately, it's becoming more difficult."

Anu listened carefully, intrigued by the direction the conversation was heading, as he served the next dosa and poured batter onto the pan for the next one. Inara showed no sign of finishing her meal anytime soon.

"Now, unlike those usual stories, I've decided to display my power to the world. To do some real good," she said, still focused on her dosa, not bothering to gauge his reaction.

Anu raised an eyebrow, intrigued. "So, what? You want to be a superhero? Fight crime?"

Inara laughed softly, shaking her head. "No! But yes, I am going to fight crime. I can make a difference in the world because I have no desire for power, money, or personal gain. I'm immune to the temptations that corrupt others." Her eyes sparkled with a determined gleam. "That's why I've decided to enter politics."

Anu, shocked, looked deep into her eyes. "Politics?"

"Yes," Inara said, her voice calm but resolute. "I'm going to run for Prime Minister of India."

"I've lived long enough to see the cycles of history, the rise and fall of leaders, and the mistakes humanity continues to make. But I believe I can change things for the better. Since I'm an immortal, who has no personal agenda, I can focus on what's best for the people. I can start here in India, and from there… who knows?"

Anu was speechless for a moment, trying to process everything. "So, you think by becoming Prime Minister, you can... what? Fix the world?"

Inara smiled, a glimmer of hope in her eyes. "I can try. I'll bring about changes that no politician, bound by the desires for wealth and power, could ever achieve. With time on my side, I can ensure progress is made, not for short-term gains, but for the long-term benefit of humanity."

Anu leaned back, shaking his head in disbelief. "And here I thought you just wanted help writing a book."

Inara laughed softly. "No, Anu. My story is far from over. In fact…" She straightened up gracefully, her figure framed by the window behind her. "A new story begins. And this time, it won't be fiction. It's going to make history."

Anu couldn't shake the feeling that this was just the beginning—that Inara's request was far more than a casual favor. He wasn't sure how he fit into her plan, but the weight of her words, her calm certainty, made it clear that whatever came next would be anything but simple. As she finished her dosa and looked up at him with that same easy smile, Anu felt a subtle unease stir within him.

There was something unspoken in her eyes—something deeper. For the first time, he wondered if even Inara, with all her power, knew exactly where this path would lead.

OTHER WORK BY THE AUTHOR

In a world overflowing with endless advice and complicated paths to peace, The One Rule for Peace offers a refreshingly

simple solution. This brief yet profound book holds the key to lasting serenity and fulfillment through one simple, powerful rule.

It's not about complexity but the elegance of simplicity. This book challenges how you view your life and the choices you make, offering a minimalist guide to achieving clarity in a chaotic world. Sometimes, the answers are far simpler than we expect.

The One Rule for Peace is a concise, thought-provoking read, perfect for anyone seeking calm and insight in its purest form.

Available on Amazon in both Kindle and Paperback formats.

FUTURE BOOKS FROM THE AUTHOR

VILLAIN FOREVER: LEGACY OF INARA

Inara, an immortal who has seen empires rise and fall, has spent centuries watching humanity repeat its mistakes. Now, she's stepping into the light, determined to become the Prime Minister of India and bring lasting change to the world plagued by corruption and short-sighted leadership.

Immune to power's usual temptations, Inara believes her immortality gives her a unique perspective—one that can reshape the future. But as she navigates the treacherous world of politics, she faces a daunting question: will she transform the system or be transformed by it? Will Inara step down gracefully after achieving her goals, or will the pull of power be too strong even for an immortal?

Inara's legacy is uncertain, but one thing is clear: this is a story of power, immortality, and the fine line between hero and villain.

THE KUMBAKONAM EXPRESS

In The Kumbakonam Express, a group of reality show pranksters plans their most daring stunt yet—a staged hijacking of the train. What begins as a lighthearted joke quickly spirals out of control when a high-ranking central minister on board misinterprets the prank as a real terror attack. The military is called in, and the pranksters suddenly find themselves facing a very real fight for survival.

As the situation escalates, the innocent team becomes trapped in a deadly political conspiracy. Manipulated by powerful forces seeking to exploit the chaos for their own gain, the group must navigate a terrifying reality where their lives are at stake, and no one is who they seem.

The Kumbakonam Express is a gripping political thriller where a prank hijack turns into a desperate struggle for survival, with the truth buried beneath layers of political intrigue.

THE WHITEFIELD ROAD

On a regular day in the bustling city of Bangalore, nothing seems out of the ordinary—until one voice on the radio changes everything. A once-beloved radio jockey, now disillusioned and furious with the world around her, takes to the airwaves with a message of chaos. But this time, she's not just broadcasting—she's hijacking the people of Whitefield Road, a key artery of the city.

Using her platform and her inside knowledge of the city's pulse, she manipulates the crowd, inciting confusion, fear, and frenzy. But who is she really angry at? Is it the corrupt system, the apathetic listeners, or the powerful individuals who silenced her voice? With a cryptic agenda and a deep-rooted vendetta, she turns the street into a battleground, leaving the authorities—and the public—scrambling to piece together her twisted plan.

The Whitefield Road is a gripping psychological thriller where a voice meant to entertain becomes one of terror, and a city's everyday commute becomes a fight for control. What happens when the people themselves become the target?

<h1 style="text-align:center">EYES ALWAYS LIE</h1>

In Eyes Always Lie, a perfectly executed bank robbery leaves authorities baffled—not because of how it was done, but because every single robber is now dead, having taken their own lives. Even stranger, there is no apparent connection between the robbers. They came from different walks of life, some living successful, seemingly perfect lives. And yet, the money is missing, and the answers are nowhere to be found.

As their friends and families remain oblivious to the dark secrets that led them to this deadly heist, detective Inara is called in to untangle the web of mystery. Who was behind this masterfully orchestrated plan? What kind of power did the mastermind hold over these individuals that forced them to commit the crime—and end their own lives?

Eyes Always Lie is a twisted psychological thriller where every clue leads to more questions, and the truth hides behind the most innocent of faces. Can Inara uncover the mastermind before more lives are lost?

THE HEART OF A LYING

The Heart of a Lying traces the journey of a man who has spent his life lying—not out of selfishness, but from a complex, almost tragic, selflessness. Since childhood, he sensed that those around him—family, friends, lovers—couldn't handle or understand his truths. To protect them, he began concealing his real thoughts and feelings, using lies as a bridge to connect, even if it meant sacrificing authenticity.

Over forty years, this choice casts a shadow over his life, leading to failed relationships and persistent loneliness. Though a few friends accept his evasions, no one truly understands him. He begins to question whether his lies were genuinely selfless or a quiet form of self-protection, rooted in a fear of losing the fragile connections he's worked to keep.

Caught between the desire to belong and the need to shield his true self, he longs for someone who could accept him, lies and all. The Heart of a Lying is a poignant exploration of the fine line between selflessness and self-protection—and the profound isolation that comes when hiding who you truly are.

PASSION, LUCK, AND WHAT THE …

From a young age, a boy dreams of designing aircraft to fight bad guys and make the world a safer place, inspired by the heroic cartoons he watches. Despite his family's skepticism, he holds tight to his vision, nurturing his fascination with aviation. Against the odds, he earns a place at one of India's top universities for aerospace engineering, where his dedication and a bit of good fortune propel him forward.

After completing his master's, he joins India's aeronautics company, a step that marks the beginning of an unexpected journey. Through a series of lucky breaks, he soon finds himself working for a global leader in aerospace—a position that seemed like a distant fantasy to the young boy he once was.

This story captures his passion and how moments of luck, paired with determination, helped him advance in the field he loves. It's a tale of how dreams take shape, even if life, in its own way, keeps a few chapters unwritten.

STAY CONNECTED WITH PeTiTe

Thank you for joining me on this journey through PeTiTe! If you'd like to share your thoughts, discuss ideas, or connect with other readers, you're welcome to follow PeTiTe on social media.

Instagram: @petite_thebook
Facebook: @petitethebook

Scan the QR codes below to join the conversation and share your reflections with the PeTiTe community.

PETITE-THE BOOK

PETITE_THEBOOK

www.ingramcontent.com/pod-product-compliance
Lightning Source LLC
La Vergne TN
LVHW091449190726
843491LV00007B/1941